To †
Happy &
Mary White
11-19-16

THE MYSTICAL MAGIC OF
MR. JINGLE

12-25-16

Kane
Have fun!! I love you
Grandma Clokaugh

Mary White

PAGE PUBLISHING, INC.
New York, NY

First originally published by Page Publishing, Inc. 2014

ISBN 978-1-63417-291-2 (pbk)
ISBN 978-1-63417-292-9 (digital)

Printed in the United States of America

I would like to dedicate this book to the Republic Middle School students in Republic, Missouri. Cartooning is a comforting stress reliever for me and some of the middle school students challenged me to step out of my comfort zone and write a book for them. Some asked me to write a book about bullying and others asked me to write an adventure story. I decided to combine the two. I hope you have as much fun reading this book as I did writing it. You are my inspiration.

CHAPTER 1

THE FIRST ENCOUNTER

As the sun began to glow over the rooftops, a gentle breeze blew back the curtain, allowing a tiny beam of light to shine into an otherwise very dark room. The alarm clock rang, and Jimmy awakens from a sound sleep. He stretches, yawns, and jumps out of bed.

He knows that today is the day of the ninjas and that he must be ready to defend his family at all cost. He brushes his teeth and gets dressed while keeping vigil to the many dangers that might be lurking in the shadows. Dressed in his white karate gi and black belt, he jumps from his bedroom into the hallway.

He looks to the left and quickly to the right. *Good, nothing's there!* he thought. He knows, however, that he can't trust fate to protect his family; it's up to him. He carefully slithers to the top of the staircase, where he sees three black ninjas; they seem to appear from nowhere. It's time to defend his country, his family, and himself. After all, this is what he has been training for his entire life.

With a running dropkick, he knocks two of the ninjas down the stairs, and a left hook to the jaw renders the third ninja virtually useless. Two more ninjas appear behind him, but he sees their shadow on the wall. He spins with another left hook and a dropkick. This time he felt a blow to the top of his head and said "Ouch, that hurt" as his brain snapped back into reality.

He heard a familiar voice saying, "Why did you kick me, you little nerd?" It was the voice of his older brother, Russ, and he knew he'd been busted. Russ was the ninja that smacked Jimmy on the head. "OK," said Jimmy. "We might as well just go to school!" He thought to himself, however, *Maybe there really will be ninjas in our house after school, and I will still be ready.*

The school bus was running on time, and Jimmy's daydreaming made them nearly miss it. By the time they boarded the bus, all the good seats in the back were filled. Russ and Jimmy had to be seated in the front of the bus. Russ turned to Jimmy and said, "Thanks for making us late, you little dork."

Jimmy had always looked up to his big brother and couldn't understand why Russ gave him such a hard time. He had noticed other high school boys protecting their little brothers. So why didn't Russ want to protect him? Was he really so weird? He knew he was a dreamer, but his biggest dream was fitting in and pleasing Russ. He knew that was never going to happen, so all he had were his dreams.

Jimmy went straight to his locker to get his books for first hour. He hoped he could get to his classroom before being spotted by the jerks that liked to pick on him. He didn't get that lucky. Austin Brady was not only the biggest kid in school but also the meanest. He sure liked picking on Jimmy and had no trouble getting others to help him.

Today was no different! When Jimmy got to the end of the lockers, a big hand reached out and grabbed him by the collar. "Where do you think you're going?" asked Austin. Jimmy just closed his eyes and cringed, knowing that nothing good was going to come out of this encounter.

Austin took Jimmy's book bag and dumped everything onto the floor. Jimmy's lunch money fell out and was grabbed up by the bullies before he could get it. This wasn't the first time they had taken his money, and he knew it wouldn't be the last.

They dragged him back to his locker, put him inside, and closed the door. Austin whispered through the holes in the door, warning Jimmy what would happen if he told on them. The only defense he had against these bullies was his imagination. He imagined all the things he would do to them once he really did learn karate.

All of a sudden, he heard footsteps coming up the hall. He wasn't sure who it was but knew his only chance of escape was to get their attention. Just as a shadow passed in front of the door, Jimmy said, "Who's there? Can you please let me out?" He heard a voice on the other side of the door say, "What in the world are you doing in there?"

He recognized the voice. It was Mr. Bowman, the principal. How was he going to explain this without telling on Austin? He knew what would happen if he told the truth, so he lied and told Mr. Bowman he didn't see who put him in the locker.

He was thirty minutes late in getting to his first-hour class and found himself being reprimanded by the teacher, Mr. Kendall. "If you can't get to my class on time," demanded Mr. Kendall, "don't come at all!" Jimmy didn't know what to say without implicating Austin. He knew that would be suicide, so he chose to say nothing at all. He vowed to himself to get even someday, and once again, his imagination began to take over.

Out of the shadows steps another black ninja. It's Austin, and the only one that can stop him is Jimmy. This time things will be different; this time he will win! Jimmy jumps up and challenges Austin to a duel and says, "This time we take no prisoners. We duel to the death."

Austin accepts the duel and jumps out the window into the court-yard, where he awaits Jimmy's arrival. Jimmy carefully maneuvers his way down the hall, knowing very well that Austin would never fight alone. He knows there will be others waiting to ambush him. *I will be ready for them*, thinks Jimmy. *I will defeat them all!*

Just as Jimmy enters the courtyard, he notices two more black ninjas hiding behind the fountain. *How many more are there? Will I be able to defeat them all?* These are the questions going through Jimmy's brain. He knows, however, that if he lets even one negative thought enter his mind, he will surely lose the battle.

He takes the stance and motions for Austin to approach. As Austin approaches from the front, the other two approach from each side. Jimmy takes out Austin first with a frontal kick; he jumps in the air, doing the splits, and gets the other two ninjas in the jaw. "Yes!" says Jimmy. "I did it."

"You did what?" asked Mr. Kendall. Once again, Jimmy's been busted, and he looked up to see a very angry teacher. Mr. Kendall said, "I asked you a question, young man. Are you going to answer or not?"

"I'm sorry," replied Jimmy. "What was your question?"

Mr. Kendall retorted, "The question is written on the board, Jimmy. Do you have the answer or not?"

"I don't know," said Jimmy. "Can I please take it home and give it to you tomorrow?" Mr. Kendall asked, "What am I going to do with you, young man? We have three days left of school, and finals start tomorrow."

Jimmy pleaded, "I'll be ready, please, Mr. Kendall, just one more chance."

Mr. Kendall bellowed, "Last chance, young man, last chance and I mean it. Go home and study—study hard!"

Jimmy made it to the end of the day. He was tired, hungry, and thoroughly fed up. The minute he got home, he raided the refrigerator and went to his room to study for finals. As he was studying, once again, his mind started wandering away into another world. He fought hard to push this world away, but it was hard to resist this wonderful world of dreams.

This was a world of ninjas, dragons, and all of the things that did not exist in the real world—the things that boys dreamed about but never really got to see. It may have been a dream world, but to Jimmy, it seemed so real. He saw himself as a man—one that was strong, not the boy that was weak and stolen from. Someday, he would be this man, but for now he had to study for finals.

Jimmy didn't keep his head in the classroom long enough to take many notes. He now had to read his books and try to make sense out of them before morning. He was failing in almost every class and knew this was his last chance to redeem himself. He needed to bring those grades up one whole point if he even wanted to pass with Ds.

Jimmy continued to read into the wee hours of the morning, constantly fighting back the urges to reminisce about becoming a white ninja. He was still at his desk, studying, when the sun came up. After a quick shower, he grabbed an egg sandwich and was off to school for finals.

Jimmy surprised himself by actually knowing the answers to many of the questions on the final exam. The last portion of the test was an essay, and he got to pick any topic he wanted to write about. "Wow, I can do this," thought Jimmy. "All I have to do is let my imagination run wild and take notes." That was exactly what he did, and before he knew it, his essay was complete, and so were the final exams. Now, all that was left was waiting for grade cards to find out if he would have to repeat the fifth grade.

He was so glad when the final bell rang for the day. Tomorrow would be the last day of school! No more exams and only one more day to put up with Austin and his friends. As soon as the bell rang, he ran as fast as he could to get on the bus before Austin spotted him. After he was seated on the bus, he noticed Austin on the sidewalk, pacing back and forth, making gestures like he wanted to fight.

Jimmy jumps out of the window, landing on Austin and knocking him to the ground. Austin jumps up, but Jimmy kicks him on the left side of his head and lands another kick to his stomach. Austin bends over and starts to cry. That's when the bus started moving and Jimmy woke up still in the safety of his seat. He just smiled at Austin as the bus pulled away.

As soon as Russ and Jimmy got home, they ran into the house, jumping over the back of the couch, wrestling for the remote. Russ got the remote, laughed at Jimmy, and said, "What did you expect, you little nerd?"

"Nothing," retorted Jimmy, "nothing from you anyway," and he went to his room in tears.

Jimmy was distraught and confused! All he could think about was why his brother didn't like him. He just knew he couldn't be that bad! *Anyway*, thought Jimmy, *school is out tomorrow, and I'll have all summer to show Russ I'm really not a nerd.*

Early the next morning, Jimmy jumped into the shower, dressed, and was off to meet the bus. *No time for dreaming today*, thought Jimmy. He just wanted to get the day over with. He was sure he had aced the finals and was so anxious to find out how he had done. Unfortunately, his anxiety caused him to let down his guard.

Today he wasn't running to escape capture but was instead walking quite leisurely down the hall. All students should have been able to take a leisurely stroll, but with bullies like Austin around, Jimmy couldn't afford leisure, and today it would cost him dearly.

He turned a corner and met Austin head-on. The reality of the situation hit him like a ton of bricks, and he knew he was in trouble. Austin reached out and grabbed Jimmy by his backpack, lifting him off the ground. Jimmy was thrashing around lashing out in an attempt at fighting back. Try as he might, Austin was too big, and Jimmy was like putty in his hands. Once again, he just closed his eyes and awaited his fate.

Luckily, fate smiled on Jimmy when Mr. Kendall stepped into the hall and saw the scuffle. "What's going on down there?" asked Mr. Kendall.

Austin turned and said, "Jimmy fell and I'm helping him up." He glared at Jimmy and whispered, "Isn't that right, Jim?" Jimmy knew he had better not push his luck, so he just said, "Right."

It was finally fifth hour, and Jimmy got handed his grade card. Two Cs and three Ds! "Yes!" said Jimmy. "I passed fifth grade!" Now, this was good news for Jimmy, but what were his parents going to say? *Oh well, this year is over, and I can't change it now*, thought Jimmy.

He knew Austin would be watching for him since he had gotten out so lucky that morning. He had become pretty good at hiding behind other kids as they walked down the hall to get on the bus. Today was no exception. He ducked down and hid behind and ran around other kids until he reached his bus.

Just as he stepped onto the bus, Austin yanked him backward and pushed him to the ground. Once again, fate smiled on Jimmy when the bus driver stepped off the bus and pulled Austin off him. He made Austin leave, helped Jimmy to his feet, and told him to get on the bus and sit down. *How great it would be if I could protect others like the bus driver protected me*, thought Jimmy.

As soon as the bus stopped in front of their house, both Jimmy and Russ jumped off the bus, shouting, "Yay, summer vacation!" and ran home. They were starving, as usual, and went directly to the refrigerator for a snack. No homework. Just the PlayStation and television until their parents got home from work.

The boys put their grade cards on the table and disappeared into the family room for an evening of games and relaxation. It wasn't long until Mom popped her head around the corner and said, "Turn off the television and come to the kitchen, boys."

Russ said, "That was quick. Must be takeout."

When the boys got to the kitchen, they knew something was wrong. No food on the table made it apparent that dinner wasn't the reason for the meeting. Mom turned to Jimmy and said, "I got a phone call from Mr. Kendall today. He is very concerned about your ability to pay attention in class. He said you're a dreamer and unable to keep your mind on a subject."

"Tell me son," said Dad. "What should we do about this situation?"

Jimmy replied, "What do you want from me? I passed all my classes!"

"We want you to do better than just pass a class," snapped Dad. "Cs and Ds are not even average, and we want better than average."

"Your grandmother asked if you could spend the summer with her in Salem. Your father and I agree it is best for you," stated Mom.

"Wow!" replied Jimmy. "I have a grandmother in Salem? Who is she and why haven't I met her?"

Russ interrupted, "Because she is as weird as you are."

Jimmy didn't hear anything Russ had to say. All he could think about was a grandmother he didn't even know existed. Why had he not heard about her before? Jimmy jumped up and asked, "When are we leaving for Salem?"

"We're not," answered dad. "You're going by bus. We've already purchased the ticket, and you leave in the morning."

Jimmy was so excited that he didn't even stay to eat dinner. He ran upstairs and started packing his suitcase in preparation for his journey. His excitement lasted just long enough for Russ to walk into his room. Russ put his hands on each side of Jimmy's face and looked him straight in the eyes. "Why do you think you never met this grandmother?" asked Russ.

"I don't know," replied Jimmy. "Do you?"

Russ said, "I've heard Mom and Dad talking, and Mom said Gram is an eccentric old woman. She lives all alone on five hundred acres of land and never has visitors."

"Well," retorted Jimmy, "that's not entirely true. She did invite me. You're just jealous 'cause she didn't ask you!"

"Yeah, right," said Russ. "No way I would want to spend any time with that crazy old woman!"

Jimmy started pacing the floor, walking in circles. He didn't know what to think. "Maybe I should ask Dad," said Jimmy. "In fact, I'm going to talk to him right now." He was sure his dad always knew what to do and would never let anyone hurt him. He ran downstairs and went directly to Dad's study. There he was, laid back in his favorite chair, reading the newspaper.

Jimmy sat down on a small table next to Dad's chair and just gazed at him. Dad lowered the newspaper and gazed back at Jimmy. "All right, what do you want?" asked Dad.

"Tell me about my grandmother," said Jimmy. "Tell me, Dad, why have I never met her before now?"

Dad had a solemn look on his face, and his eyes began to tear. "She's my mother, and I can't tell you much about her because she is a mystery even to me." His mind seemed to wander off as he told the story of his childhood and how his mother would lock herself in a room upstairs for days. When she would finally come out, she acted as if she had only been gone for a short time.

Others in the family said she was a dreamer and could never keep her mind on the important things in life. Dad looked at Jimmy and said, "She's my mother and I love her. I can tell you that her dreams have made her a very wealthy woman. She put her dreams to work by turning them into books. That's how she paid for the farm she lives on today."

"So, Dad," asked Jimmy, "why me?"

"Because you're a dreamer like her, and she thinks she can help you," answered dad.

Jimmy leaned in a little closer to his dad and asked, "So I have nothing to worry about, right?"

Dad started laughing, turned to Jimmy, and whispered in his ear, "She's a recluse, not a murderer."

Jimmy smiled and said, "OK, then. I'm packed and ready to go."

Early the next morning, Jimmy rushed downstairs with suitcase in hand and a smile on his face. He didn't even take time to drift off into his usual dream world. Not today, this was no dream. It was the beginning of a real adventure—an adventure that no one, not even Russ or Austin, could destroy.

As soon as they arrived at the bus station, Jimmy grabbed his bag and ran to the bus. Dad could barely keep up. "I get it," said Dad. "You're eager to get away for the summer. Can't you at least act like you'll miss us a little?" He was not prepared for Jimmy's response.

"I don't know. I'm a dreamer, a misfit, and I don't belong anywhere. Maybe I belong with Gram! It sounds like we are a lot alike." Dad looked so forlorn; he couldn't believe his son felt so out of place. Jimmy turned to his dad, smiled, and said, "I will miss you a little. Tell Mom I love her," and he ran to his seat and sat down.

The bus rolled away, and Jimmy fell asleep. Soon he was in another kind of dreamworld; this one was not of his making. This dream was being controlled by the demons that haunted him. He found himself running away from something he was truly frightened of. He was running, all right, but wasn't going anywhere. The demon came closer and closer until Jimmy got a good look at him.

There was Austin in his face and another Austin and another. Jimmy's feet were stuck to the ground, and he couldn't get away. All he could do was scream, and scream he did. He screamed so loud, he woke himself. Everyone on the bus was looking at him, so he shrugged his shoulders and said, "Sorry, I was dreaming." He decided to stay awake for the rest of the trip.

It wasn't long until the bus arrived in Salem, and there was Gram waiting patiently for the passengers to unload. Their eyes met, and each knew the other. Jimmy didn't know why, but Gram did. They smiled and started talking as if they had known each other forever. Jimmy still didn't know why he was there and really didn't care.

All he knew was how comfortable and safe he felt with her. He hadn't felt this way for a very long time. He was sure this was exactly where he was supposed to be. Regardless of how comfortable he felt, he still had to ask, "Why am I here, Gram. Why did you ask for me?" Gram just smiled and said, "Soon, Jimmy, it will be very clear to you, but for now, let's just get you home!"

They turned off the main road and stopped at a large gate. Solid brick fencing went as far as Jimmy could see in both directions. A large sign above the gate read BAR S. RANCH, with NO TRESPASSING signs on both sides. Gram pushed a button on her dash, and the gate opened.

As they were driving through the gate, Jimmy asked, "What does 'Bar S.' stand for, Gram?" She smiled and said, "The *S* is for 'Staples.' That is my last name."

"Wow, mine too!" replied Jimmy.

Now Gram started really laughing and stated, "Of course it is. Your father has my last name, and you have his."

The sun was starting to set when the ranch house came into view. Jimmy looked at Gram and said, "That's huge. Do you live there by yourself?"

"I sure do," replied Gram. "I don't like having others around. They're always getting in the way!"

Jimmy frowned and responded, "But I'm here. Am I going to get in your way?"

"I hope not," said Gram. "I've been looking forward to this visit. I sure hope you don't disappoint me, young man."

Jimmy looked worried and said, "Me too!"

Gram pulled up to the front door and said, "Grab your suitcase and come on in."

The front door opened into an entryway. Another door opened, leading to a large living room with a stairway on the right. Gram said, "Take your suitcase upstairs. Your room is the second door on the left."

Jimmy didn't say a word; he just started up the stairs to find his room.

The hallway was dimly lit, so shadows were moving along the wall with each step he took. Just past the first door on the left, he noticed a shelf on the wall. A small red light suddenly appeared. The light was hypnotizing, and he couldn't take his eyes off it—that is, until his concentration was broken by a jingling noise.

He jumped back, took a deep breath, and went flying down the stairs. He ran smack-dab into Gram, nearly knocking her down. "Slow down," said Gram. "What's wrong?"

Jimmy screeched, "There's something up there that glows and jingles."

"Aww," said Gram. "I see you've met Mr. Jingles. We'll see him again in the morning, but for now, it's dinner and a good night's sleep."

CHAPTER 2

THE NINJA MASTER

When Gram put dinner on the table, Jimmy shoveled every bite in as fast as possible. "I'm going to bed," said Jimmy as he started up the stairs. He wanted to respect Gram's wishes, but there was no way he could wait until morning to check out this Mr. Jingles. What was it? Where did it come from? And why did it jingle at him? These were questions flashing through his head, and he knew he had to find some answers.

He got to the top of the stairs and looked toward the shelf where he first saw Mr. Jingles, but nothing was there. He looked up and down the hall, but he didn't see anything. "Darn," he said. "I guess I'll wait until morning after all." He was sure he wouldn't get any sleep even if he was tired. There was no way he could stop thinking about Mr. Jingles.

For the first time in his life, he wasn't dreaming about fighting ninjas and saving the world. The only thing bouncing around in his head were more questions about this mysterious Mr. Jingles. But ques-

17

tions or not, he was just too tired and fell asleep within seconds of his head hitting the pillow.

Before he knew it, the sun rose and morning was at hand. His eyes opened, and the first thing on his mind was Mr. Jingles. Once again, he jumped straight out of bed and planted both feet firmly on the floor. But this time, it wasn't to fight ninjas or defeat his enemies. No. Today his excitement came from knowing he was going to meet Mr. Jingles, and his heart raced with excitement.

He was calling out for Gram as he flew down the stairs. Gram met him when he hit the bottom of the staircase and said, "You better slow down and breathe before you pass out."

"I'll be fine," replied Jimmy. "I just want to meet Mr. Jingles! Can I, Gram? You promised. Remember?"

"Yes, of course, I remember," answered Gram, "and you will, right after we eat breakfast."

"I'm too excited to eat. Please, Gram, you promised!"

"Yes, I did, and you will" was Gram's response. "This is going to be a very long day, and you need your nourishment, so first we eat."

"Oh, all right," said a very disappointed Jimmy. "Breakfast first."

Back home, he was lucky to get a bowl of cereal, but this morning he sat down to a huge stack of pancakes, bacon, eggs, and a banana. "I think I died and went to heaven," said Jimmy. "This has to be the best breakfast ever, and I just got real hungry."

"Good, you're going to need it," replied Gram. "I know you have a lot of questions about Mr. Jingles," said Gram. "I will answer as many of them as I can."

"OK," replied Jimmy as questions started pouring out of his mouth. "Where did he come from? Why did he jingle at me? Does he know me?"

"Wait a minute," said Gram. "One question at a time, please."

"I'm sorry," answered Jimmy. "Can you at least tell me where he came from?"

Gram started shaking her head and said, "That's the one thing I can't tell you because I don't know. He has been in our family for generations, but only a few of us know about him."

"But I know about him," stated Jimmy. "Why did you choose to tell me, Gram?"

"I didn't choose you, Jimmy. Mr. Jingles chose you," replied Gram. "I make sure Mr. Jingles meets every grandchild born into the family, but you are the first one he has shown himself to. That means he has chosen you."

Jimmy's heart was about to pound out of his chest. He jumped out of his chair and asked, "Chosen me for what?"

Gram smiled and answered, "He has chosen you to go on the biggest adventure of your life, and that adventure starts today."

"Oh, Gram," cried Jimmy. "Can I meet Mr. Jingles now? Please, Gram, I'm ready for my adventure. I promise."

"Yes, Jimmy," said Gram. "It's time for you to meet Mr. Jingles."

Gram reached into her apron pocket and pulled out an object that resembled a bell that had been stepped on and flattened. It was difficult to tell what held the bell-shaped top and the flat bottom together. Gram held the object in the palm of her hand, stretched her arm out toward Jimmy, and said, "Meet Mr. Jingles."

When Jimmy leaned forward to get a better look, a bright red light started glowing from inside the object, and it started jingling. The jingling almost sounded like laughter, and this made Jimmy start laughing. Gram started laughing and said, "It's time for your adventure to begin. Take my other hand, Jimmy, and close your eyes." He took her hand, closed his eyes, and started to feel like he was falling. He couldn't stop falling and couldn't open his eyes. As a matter of fact, he couldn't move at all.

It was almost like a dream until he felt his feet touch the ground and his eyes popped open. He still had a firm hold on Gram's hand, but when he turned to see if she was all right, it wasn't Gram. He was holding the hand of a young girl about his age.

He jerked away from the girl, jumped backward, and asked, "Who are you and what have you done with Gram?"

"Relax, Jimmy," replied the girl. "It's me. I am Gram."

"No way!" retorted Jimmy. "How can you possibly be my Gram when you are my age?"

"That's the magic of Mr. Jingles," answered Gram. "That's why he chose you, Jimmy. You're a dreamer, and it takes a dreamer to believe. I started my adventures with my Gramps when I was your age. Now it's your turn, and this is your adventure. You get to decide where this adventure will take us."

Jimmy was confused. He turned to Gram and whispered, "But I don't know how to find an adventure."

"Sure you do, Jimmy," replied Gram. "You're a dreamer, so take us to your dreamworld."

"Well," stated Jimmy. "I have always dreamed about meeting a real ninja master and learning karate. Maybe we should start there."

"Perfect," replied Gram as she put Mr. Jingles into Jimmy's hand. "Now close your eyes and take us to your dreamworld."

Jimmy did just that. He closed his eyes, and they started their descent into another world. Once again, he felt his feet make contact with a solid surface. He opened his eyes and found himself standing in front of a real ninja master and his students. Jimmy bowed to the master and asked, "Can you teach me?"

"Yes," said the Master as he returned the bow. "Join us and we will make you a ninja."

Jimmy and Gram were both very excited and eager to start learning. There would be no daydreaming in this class for Jimmy. He hung on every word his teacher had to say, and learn he did. Both Jimmy and Gram picked up every technique and skill so fast that Jimmy could hardly believe it himself.

One afternoon, while they were sparring in the arena, an older gentleman from the local village came running through the gates, asking to see the master. He was quickly escorted to the master's hut, where he handed the master a scroll. After reading the scroll, the master ordered his men to sound the general alarm. The alarm brought all the students to the courtyard, standing at attention.

"We have been summoned to defend the local village," said the master. "It seems like a small army of men has invaded the village. They are searching for the golden dragon and must not be allowed to find it."

The students clicked their heels together and bowed in reverence to the master. They were ready to fight to the death if that was what it came to.

Jimmy was ready to fight also, but his young age made him more curious than the others. He went to the master and asked, "What is so important about the golden dragon?" The master told him that the golden dragon holds the power of light. If it fell into the wrong hands, it could cause total darkness, and this would create chaos around the world.

"OK then," said Jimmy. "Let us go and save the golden dragon from this dreaded army." Jimmy returned to tell Gram what they were about to do, and Gram reminded him, "This is your dream, Jimmy, and you are in control. We will fight together and be victorious."

The student ninjas lined up in three rows, and the gates were opened wide for departure. The master shouted out a loud battle cry that was returned with an even louder battle cry by the students. They started a slow run toward the village, keeping in perfect rhythm and stride.

As they approached the village, they could hear screams of terror from the women as their homes were being pillaged by the enemy. Jimmy's heart was pounding with the anticipation of his first real battle. He had been picked on by bullies his entire life, and this was his big chance to retaliate. This wasn't an organized army; it was just a bunch of bullies that needed a good lesson, and he wanted to be their teacher.

The students didn't break stride as they encountered the enemy. Instead, they cleared a path, sending the enemy flying in all directions. Gram and Jimmy were hitting, kicking, throwing, and knocking out every enemy they came in contact with. By the time they reached the other end of the village, the villagers were shouting with joy. The enemy had been subdued, and the village was at peace once again.

The return from the village to the school was much more relaxed, and Jimmy's heart had gone from pounding to a feeling of pride and confidence. He knew he would always be a nerd, but even a nerd could defend against the bullies if he just had confidence. OK, maybe a little more training than confidence, but obviously, they were both important.

Back at school, the spirits were high and the students celebrated their victory. They rejoiced the rest of the day, knowing intense training would begin once more with the sunrise. They were so hyped up from their victory that it made them even more eager to start training again.

Jimmy and Gram were both very good with their technique, but not perfect. Good just wasn't good enough. They both knew they must be perfect before they could continue their journey. They were prepared to work as hard as they could to complete their education.

It was still dark out when the students assembled on the sparring field to greet the sunrise. All eyes were facing east, watching for that first flash of sunlight. That flash of light would be the signal for sparring to begin. This was the first time that all the students would be sparring at the same time.

The rule was simple. Square off with the person standing next to you, making full body contact in an attempt to throw your opponent to the ground. When one of the students fell to the ground, they would be signaled to leave the field. The student still standing would square off against another student that was still standing.

This competition would continue until only one person is left standing. The winner will be honored by getting an opportunity to spar against the grand master himself. This was indeed a rare honor, and Jimmy knew that every student there would be fighting hard to earn the honor.

Jimmy knew he had to win. For him, it was more than just an honor. This would be a chance to learn the grand master's secret to humility and self-control—two elements he needed to fully understand if he was to ever reach perfection.

A beam of light flashed over the mountains, and sparring commenced. Jimmy quickly spun to face his opponent, and they started circling while keeping constant eye contact. They were both waiting for the other to make the first move.

Jimmy faked an aggressive move, throwing his opponent off guard. The opponent lunged, but Jimmy was quicker and managed to trip him. He threw his opponent to the ground, and the first match was over. Jimmy was still standing. He helped his opponent get on his feet and bowed in respect to him.

Students were being eliminated one by one until only the victors remained on the field. Jimmy noticed that Gram had been victorious and remained on the field with him. He smiled and bowed to her and then took his position to square off against another opponent.

He looked up and made eye contact with his new opponent. He had sparred against this one before and lost because he had not yet developed enough hand speed. That was then and this is now, and Jimmy was pretty sure things were going to turn out differently this time.

The second round would begin with the third sounding of the battle horn. First, second, third, and the battle began. A hand flew at Jimmy with lightning speed but, this time; Jimmy was faster and blocked the blow. Hands were flying with unbelievable speed from both sides with each being blocked by the other. It was apparent this was a very good match and both were excellent fighters.

It was inevitable; however, eventually, only one would stand victorious. All the other battles were over, and Jimmy was still fighting his opponent. All the other students gathered around to watch this magnificent display of skills. All of the sudden, Jimmy's opponent made a mistake, allowing Jimmy to deliver a powerful kick to the jaw, knocking his opponent to the ground.

Only five students remained on the field of battle: Jimmy, Gram, and three others. It was decided that Gram would spar against one and Jimmy would spar against two. For Jimmy, this was the ultimate test of his ability to control any situation, and after all, that was exactly why he was there.

They were told to take a short pause before the next battle. This gave Gram and Jimmy a chance to visit and plan their line of attack for the next battle. They also discussed what they would do if they were the last two standing. "Don't worry about the last battle," said Gram. "Let's just get through this battle, and if we both win, I will take care of it."

Just then, the alarm sounded for them to prepare for battle. Everyone returned to the arena and took their places in anticipation of this round. Once again, the fight would launch at the third sounding of the battle horn. First, second, third and the battle commenced.

Since Jimmy was sparring against two, they were much more aggressive, assuming they had the upper hand. Jimmy had paid close attention to the words of the master and learned quickly to defend against more than one aggressor. A highly skilled ninja finds two enemies easier to handle than one. This was no exception, and Jimmy put one of the opponents on the ground within the first thirty seconds of play.

For the first time in Jimmy's life, he understood the meaning of confidence. He wasn't frightened and certainly not intimidated. He found himself more like a cat playing with a mouse. He was actually finding himself quite entertained by simply holding off the attacks of his opponent.

One of the basic rules of fighting is to wear down your opponent rendering him too tired to continue. It was, however, time to end this bout, so Jimmy grabbed his opponent's right arm and firmly planted his left foot into the student's jaw. Down he went, game over and the end of this bout.

Two left standing—Gram and Jimmy. Gram bowed to the master and begged permission to forfeit the game. "We are family," she said. "Families fight for each other, not against each other."

"If that is what you want, I will honor your wishes," replied the master. He said he would be honored if they both joined him for the evening's meal.

"That would be great!" said Jimmy with an abundant amount of enthusiasm. He quickly regained his composure and said, "I mean, yes, sir, we would be honored." The master laughingly said, "Good. See you at six o'clock," and walked away. Jimmy was ecstatic—a private meeting with the three of them. He was sure nothing could be better than that.

Gram knocked on Jimmy's door at a quarter to six. "Are you ready to go?" she asked.

Jimmy opened the door and said, "Are you kidding? I was ready an hour ago. So what took you so long?"

She just laughed and said, "I just look ten years old. I'm really sixty-eight, remember?"

By now they were both laughing, and Jimmy remarked, "Oh yes, I forgot because you not only look good, you also fight really well."

Gram just laughed and said, "That's the magic of Mr. Jingles."

When they arrived outside the main dining room doors, two heavily armed guards stepped aside and motioned for them to enter. When they entered the room, the master was already seated. He motioned for them to join him at his table. They walked over, bowed, and sat down.

Both Gram and Jimmy sat very quietly during dinner, listening intently while soaking up every word the master had to say. Jimmy was sure this was the wisest man in the world, and he was determined to learn from him. The master was just as eager to teach.

They enjoyed the evening very much, but the meal was finished and time ran out. The master stood up, bowed, and said, "I will see you at the sunrise, Master Jimmy. We will spar at first light."

"Yes, most certainly, master. We shall meet at first light," replied Jimmy as he stood and returned the bow.

On the way back to their rooms, Jimmy started laughing and asked Gram if she had noticed how much bowing was going on around there. "Sure have," answered Gram. "And I am so proud of the respect you have shown to the master by returning his bow."

"Yes, and maybe that's the magic of Mr. Jingles too," responded Jimmy.

Gram started laughing, and as she rubbed the back of her hand across Jimmy's cheek, she said, "I love you, Jimmy. See you in the morning."

Jimmy loved his Mom and Dad very much, but between working and always having to yell at him for being such a dreamer and a silly twit, they just never got around to saying "I love you."

It was a wonderful feeling to just hear Gram say that. He knew he loved her too, and there was nothing he wouldn't do for her. As his head lay back on the pillow, he smiled and mumbled oh so quietly, "Thank you, Mr. Jingles," and fell asleep.

The next thing he heard was Gram pounding on the door. "Wake up, Jimmy. It's almost sunrise!"

He flew out of bed, rushing toward the bathroom while yelling back, "I'll be right out!" He ran the brush through his hair once and splashed water on his face four or five times, and he was running out the door.

"I'm on it," said Jimmy as they were both running toward the sparring field. This was one of the most important days in Jimmy's life, and he didn't want to be late. Just as they arrived at the gate to the field, the signal for all to assemble went off, and Jimmy noticed that the master was just arriving himself.

He was relieved to know all was well and he had time to spare. Jimmy and the master walked to the center of the field while all the others gathered around, standing at attention. The grand master said, "First, we practice patience and stretch in unison."

The master would usually watch, but today he would lead. He started gliding effortlessly from one position to another with smooth, almost motionless power. It seemed as if his power of thought had over taken the will of everyone on the field. They were also flowing through the same motions.

Jimmy, too, was going through all the motions, and even though the master's lips were not moving, Jimmy could hear his words. "True strength and courage does not come from teaching. It comes from within." And all of a sudden, the spell was over. For a second, there was a still, almost eerie silence that passed over the field.

Then a loud, warrior's cry echoed throughout the field, and it was time for sparring. This match would be a demonstration of stick fighting, a form of Japanese fighting called kendo. The bamboo sticks simulate swords and are used as safe training methods for dangerous weapons.

Jimmy cleared his mind of any thoughts of the outside world. He wanted to absorb every ounce of knowledge being passed to him by the master. No words were being spoken, yet Jimmy was learning second by second. It was as if the master was draining his knowledge into Jimmy. When he became proficient in the art of kendo, time was called and this round was over.

Each round that followed went the same as the first until Jimmy was proficient in every aspect of martial arts. He bowed to the master and heard a voice deep within say, "A true ninja does not fight for the sake of fighting. He fights for truth and justice."

The master bowed and said, "You have learned all that I can teach you, my son. It is time for you to leave." Jimmy realized Gram was standing beside him. She reached out and took his hand. He felt himself floating downward until, once again, his feet touched solid ground. His eyes opened, and he was back at the ranch.

He looked to see if Gram was with him, and once again, he was astonished with what he saw. He hadn't returned with a ten-year-old girl but a sixty-eight-year-old grandmother. As curious as he was, he found himself much too tired to ask questions now. He felt himself floating up the stairs and into his bed. He was asleep before his head hit the pillow.

CHAPTER 3

THE CATTLE DRIVE

The next day, Jimmy slept until almost noon. When he finally woke up, he was so weak, he could hardly get out of bed. After his shower, he wiped the mirror clean and realized he wasn't so scrawny anymore. He actually saw muscle appearing on his chest and arms. He thought the whole experience had been a dream, but dreams didn't build muscle. *It wasn't a dream*, thought Jimmy. *That means Mr. Jingles is real.*

He was filled with excitement and started downstairs to find Gram. He heard dishes clinking in the kitchen and headed that direction. He was yelling, "Gram, it's really real. We did those things!"

Gram popped her head around the corner and replied, "It certainly is real Jimmy, and right now, you need to eat and build back your strength."

When he saw the breakfast Gram had prepared, his eyes widened in amazement. The table was stacked high with bacon, pancakes, eggs, cinnamon rolls, milk, juice, and fruit. Jimmy looked at Gram and asked, "How many people are coming for breakfast?"

"It's just the two of us," answered Gram. "I think you'll find this is just enough to make you feel stronger."

As soon as Jimmy started eating, he realized just how hungry he was. "I can't ever remember food tasting this good or feeling this hungry," remarked Jimmy.

"That's because we didn't eat or sleep the entire time we were gone," replied Gram.

"How is that possible?" asked Jimmy. "We must have been gone for weeks."

"No," answered Gram. "We were gone for three days"

"Three days?"exclaimed Jimmy. "It seemed so much longer."

Once again Gram smiled and said, "That's the magic of Mr. Jingles."

Jimmy hadn't eaten this much food in his entire life, but Gram was right: the more he ate, the stronger and better he felt. Soon the table was empty and Jimmy was stronger than ever, and he asked, "When do we get to go again?"

"Soon," answered Gram, "but first we have to rest up and tend to chores on the farm."

"Chores?" screeched Jimmy. "Nobody said anything about chores."

Gram laughed and responded, "Well then, who's going to take care of all the cows and horses?"

"Horses?" asked Jimmy as his head turned toward Gram. "You have horses?"

"Yes," answered Gram. "We have horses, and right now, we have to make sure they have plenty of food and water."

"All right," said Jimmy. "Nobody said anything about horses either."

When they went out the back door, Jimmy paused to admire how beautiful the farm was. There were really big barns, smaller barns, and several outbuildings. A white wood fence behind the barns went in both directions as far as he could see. Behind the fence were beautiful rolling pastures that appeared to end at a tree line.

He didn't, however, see any animals. "Where are all the horses?" he asked. "I don't see any horses, and come to think about it, I don't see any cows either!"

Gram answered with a smile, "No, you don't. They are beyond that tree line and down the bluff in the old pasture. They like to graze down there because a spring-fed creek runs right down the middle of the pasture, keeping the grass green and plush."

"Come on," said Gram. "Let's go get a tractor from the barn and take a bale of hay to the horses."

"Tractor?" said Jimmy. "Nobody said anything about a tractor either. Can I drive it? Well, can I?"

"Wait a minute and slow down there," said Gram. "How about we do this together?" Gram opened the large sliding barn doors, and Jimmy looked inside.

He didn't see *a* tractor. He saw *a lot* of tractors in a lot of different sizes. "Good grief!" exclaimed Jimmy. "How many tractors do you have?" Before Gram could answer him, he said, "Looks like we can both take a tractor."

"You can take any tractor you want, Jimmy," replied Gram, "just as soon as I teach you how to drive it." He thought to himself, *This is the best summer ever.*

Gram crawled aboard the biggest tractor, turned the key, and a puff of black smoke came billowing out of the smoke stack. "Come on up," said Gram as she patted the seat beside her. She had levers at her feet and levers at her hands, and she was moving them all. She explained what each lever controlled and asked if he was ready. He nodded his head yes.

The tractor took off, and they were on their way to get a big round bale of hay. Jimmy had never been on a tractor and was awed by the experience. He had the wind blowing through his hair and was bouncing around all over the seat. They were traveling at least eight miles an hour across the pasture headed for the tree line.

They followed a trail that passed through the trees and ended up at a steep bluff. "That sure looks steep," said Jimmy.

Gram just laughed and shouted, "Hang on, Jimmy, we're going for a ride!"

"Yahoo!" yelled Jimmy as they took off down the bluff. He shouted, "This is the second best thing I've done this week!" He took Gram's arm and squeezed it really tight.

"Me too, Jimmy," said Gram. "Me too."

They followed the trail down the bluff, winding around boulders and trees, until they reached the bottom. When they got leveled out, Jimmy looked up and got a glimpse of the most beautiful sight he had ever seen. He was thinking two, maybe three horses, but this was a whole herd. "Pick one and she's yours," said Gram.

"How do I pick just one? They are all so beautiful," asked Jimmy.

"Take your time. It will come to you," answered Gram.

"Okay," he said, "and if I pick one, can I put a saddle on it and take it for a ride?"

"I don't know," said Gram. "Do you know how to ride a horse?"

"Of course," replied Jimmy. "Everybody knows how to ride a horse."

"Well," smirked Gram. "Let me rephrase the question. Have you ever been on a horse?"

"Not a real one," answered Jimmy, "but I can learn if you teach me."

Gram shrugged her shoulders, smiled, and said, "I think it's time for another adventure."

"All right!" screeched Jimmy. "Let's go to a dude ranch."

Gram frowned and retorted, "A dude ranch? I think we can do better than that!"

"What's better than a dude ranch?" asked Jimmy.

Gram answered, "How about a real cattle ranch in the real old West days?"

"That's a great idea," remarked Jimmy. "When can we go?"

"After we have looked after the ranch and done all our chores," answered Gram. They dropped the bale of hay and took off across the pasture to make sure the spring and creek were clear of debris. Debris would cause a dam and stop the flow of water to the horses. Horses weren't the only animals in the lower pasture; there was also a fair-sized herd of Black Angus cattle.

Jimmy noticed one of the horses following the tractor. It was a black-and-white paint with a white face and a black circle around the left eye. When Jimmy pointed the horse out to Gram, she laughed and said, "Let's see if she follows us all the way home."

"If she does, can I keep her?" asked Jimmy.

"You sure can," answered Gram.

They wound around, following the creek, stopping just long enough to remove logs and other debris from the water. Every time they stopped, the little mare would also stop and just stand there. As the tractor pulled away, the horse started following again.

Sure enough, when they passed through the last gate into the small pasture by the house, the mare was right with them. Jimmy climbed off the tractor and closed the gate behind her. He turned to face the horse and said, "Now, I don't have to choose a horse. It seems one has chosen me!"

They pulled up to the barn, and the horse was still right on their tail. Gram remarked, "Now that you are a horse owner, you have responsibilities."

"What kind of responsibilities?" asked Jimmy.

Her reply was simple. "She's a child and you're her parent. Now you have to make sure she has plenty of food, water, and shelter."

Jimmy looked around and said, "There's plenty of food in the pasture for one horse. I will make sure the tank is full of water and she can use the lean-to coming off the side of the big barn for shelter."

"I'm impressed," remarked Gram. "Now I'm going in to fix dinner. Just make sure you talk to her before you come in for the evening."

When they sat down at the dinner table, Jimmy found himself more interested in talking to Gram than watching television or playing video games. Back home, the family rarely ate at the table, and when they did, nobody would talk.

Mom was so tired from working all day; she just wanted to go soak in a tub before bedtime. Dad would eat really fast so he could retire to his office and finish the work he brought home. Russ didn't want to eat at the table anyway. All he wanted to do was play video games.

This was an altogether different lifestyle, and Jimmy found himself talking about almost everything they had done throughout the day. They laughed about their tractor ride down the bluff and the pretty little mare that seemed to fall in love with Jimmy.

"There are a couple of things we always need to do before any adventure," stated Gram. "One of the most important things we have to do here is make sure the animals have enough food and water before we go. Since our adventures usually last three to four days, that's how many days we must prepare to be gone."

"What about people?" asked Jimmy. "How do we disappear without people knowing we're gone?"

"All you ever have to tell anyone is your job takes you away, and Mr. Jingles provides the rest," replied Gram.

"Okay," said Jimmy. "I guess I'll just face that when the time comes, but for now, it's just you and me, Gram."

"There is one more very important rule," said Gram. "You need to pay very close attention to what I'm about to tell you. Mr. Jingles is our secret, yours and mine. That means nobody else can ever know about him—not your parents, not your brother, not your friends or, someday, your wife, and not even your children.

"When you get old like me, it will be your job to let Mr. Jingles meet each of your grandchildren. He will know which one will take your place, the same as you are taking mine."

Jimmy looked worried and asked, "You're going to go on the adventures with me, aren't you, Gram?"

She hugged him really hard and answered, "I'm going to be here as long as you need me. You'll understand more before the end of summer.

"Enough serious talk for now. Let's have dessert." She opened the refrigerator and took out a chocolate cream pie. There's just something about chocolate pie that lightens a conversation and makes a person feel good. They spent the rest of the evening talking and laughing about their first adventure together.

Before they knew it, it was bedtime. Gram kissed Jimmy on the cheek and said, "Better get a good night's sleep. We leave for our next adventure right after breakfast." She got no argument out of him. It had been a long day, and he was really tired.

Jimmy must have been asleep before his head hit the pillow because the next thing he heard was Gram's voice calling out, "Breakfast is ready, sleepyhead. Time to get up." His eyes popped open, and he sat up in bed, looking around in an attempt to remember where he was. *Oh wow, I'm at Gram's.* And with that thought, he jumped out of bed.

He remembered that today was the start of a new adventure. He took off down the stairs, shouting, "I'm coming, Gram!" He knew the

35

drill: breakfast first then the adventure. "Good morning," he said as he entered the kitchen. Gram just smiled, and they both started eating. They were both anticipating the adventure that awaited them.

Breakfast was over, chores were done, and they were both ready for the adventure to begin. Jimmy took Gram's hand and said, "I'm ready. Let's go."

Gram laughed and said, "This is your adventure. Where is Mr. Jingles?" Jimmy giggled, reached in his pocket, and pulled out Mr. Jingles. "Oops, I forgot it was my turn," remarked Jimmy.

He was holding Gram's hand so tight, his fingers turned white while firmly gripping Mr. Jingles with his other hand. They closed their eyes, fell fast asleep, and started their descent. Soon their feet touched solid ground, and their eyes opened. Gram was ten years old again, but this time, there were five more kids, all around ten or eleven years old.

"Who are you guys?" asked Jimmy.

Gram answered for them. "I talked to Gramps last night and asked him to gather everyone for a cattle drive." Jimmy looked around and noticed about a hundred head of cattle and seven horses. His eyes became fixed on a black-and-white paint mare with a white face and a black circle around her left eye.

She looked identical to the little mare Gram had just given him back home. "Go on over and make friends with her. She will be your horse for the cattle drive," explained one of the boys standing there.

"Thanks," said Jimmy. "Who are you?"

The boy smiled and answered, "You can call me Pete, but Sara here, she calls me Gramps."

He was pointing to Gram, and Jimmy realized that Pete was his great-great grandfather. Jimmy extended his hand and said, "Pleased to meet you, sir."

The boy laughed and replied, "My pleasure, Jimmy, but please call me Pete."

Jimmy smiled and said, "Okay. Pete it is."

He turned and walked slowly toward the mare and asked, "What's her name?"

"She was named by the Indian that broke her. She is called Sioux Z. That is 'Sioux' for the tribal name and *Z* for 'EZ rider,'" answered Pete.

"Can I ride her?" asked Jimmy.

"That's my boy," said Pete. "Let's get saddled up and take her for a ride."

Pete was the expert horseman, so Jimmy listened intently to his every word and watched diligently his every move. He had become accustomed to learning a lot in a short period, and this was no exception. Pete taught Jimmy the proper method of saddling a horse and how to make a hackamore out of rope.

Pete explained how the Indians preferred this type of a headgear. It had no harsh bit to go in the horse's mouth, making it easier for the horse to tolerate. Jimmy liked the idea of using a hackamore on his horse. The last thing he wanted to do was make any horse uncomfortable.

They were all saddled up and ready to ride. Jimmy watched closely as Pete mounted his horse. He put his left foot in the stirrup and pushed off with his right foot, throwing his right leg over the saddle into the stirrup on the other side. "I can do that," remarked Jimmy and looked like a pro getting on a horse.

Pete taught him how to hold the reins, how to make the horse go to the right, how to go to the left, and how to make her stop. "I've got it," said Jimmy. "Let's ride." He watched as Pete leaned forward in the saddle and gently kicked his horse in the sides, and she took off running. "Let's do this," said Jimmy, and they were off to catch Pete.

They were riding like the wind across the pastures, through the creek, and over fences, stopping just long enough to give the horses a rest. Pete didn't look like a grandfather, but he sure acted like one. One minute he was criticizing Jimmy, and the next minute he was praising him. Jimmy knew he needed the criticism to make him better, but he also needed the praise to boost his confidence.

Every time they remounted, Jimmy got a little better, and as they were returning to the bunkhouse, Pete said, "I believe you're ready, Jimmy. We leave in the morning right after breakfast!" Jimmy was proud of his accomplishment. Even more important was knowing that Gram would be proud.

Everyone pitched in to build a campfire and cook a big pot of beans and bacon. Gram filled a Dutch oven with biscuits and put hot coals over the top of it. After dinner, Jimmy just sat quietly, listening to the others reminisce about their adventures. He got goose bumps every time he was reminded that it was now his turn to make the adventures.

Gram turned to Jimmy and said, "Speaking of your adventure, it starts very early. Time to say good night."

Jimmy was up before the sunrise, sneaking out to feed and brush his horse. He was talking to her like she was a friend, and she seemed to respond to his every word. He was a dreamer and a misfit in the human world, but little did he know that he would be right at home in the animal world.

He thought to himself, "Guess that's why Gram lives on a farm with lots of animals and no people." Just then, the first sign of light popped over the hills, and the bunkhouse came alive. Jimmy wasn't the only one excited about rounding up the herd and driving them to market; the others were just as excited.

Seven riders and ten horses—three packed heavy with gear and seven saddled and ready to go. "Let's ride!" shouted Pete as they mounted their horses and rode off toward the sunrise and a hundred head of cattle. It was a good thing that Jimmy learned how to ride, because he didn't know a darn thing about rounding up cattle.

He wasn't worried because in Mr. Jingle's world, learning came quickly. He still didn't know exactly who these other kids were, but it was obvious Pete was the leader and the one to learn from. When they came upon the herd, Pete told everyone to spread out and follow his lead.

When everyone was in position, Pete started swinging his rope in a circle and slapping his saddle to make noise. He yelled, "Haw! Get up there!" and everyone else followed his lead. The cattle started moving in the direction they were being led. They stopped just long enough for a quick lunch, and they were right back in the saddle, pushing the cattle at a steady pace.

Pete yelled out, "Pick up the pace, people! We want to reach the flatlands in time to set up camp." They went from a fast walk to a slow gallop, and most of the cattle went along, but a few fell behind. Pete hollered at Jimmy, "Those are yours, Jimmy! Round them in with the rest of the herd."

Jimmy spun his horse around and got behind the strays. He was swinging his rope and shouting, "Get in there, little doggie" just like a real cowboy. It made him so proud when those cows joined the rest of the herd and Pete said, "Good job, son." Gram smiled and winked at him, making him feel even better. He knew he had a lot to learn, but he sure was proud of the job he was doing.

The pace they set worked out better than expected. They reached the flatlands in plenty of time to set up camp and prepare for nightfall. Gram went over to Jimmy and said, "I hope you got a good night's sleep last night. It's the last bed you'll see for a couple of days."

Jimmy got a puzzled look on his face and asked, "Aren't we going to have beds?"

Gram laughed and answered, "Not on a cattle drive. We sleep under the stars and on the ground in sleeping bags."

Jimmy thought, *That's great. I've never slept outside before.* Then he asked, "But what will we do if it rains?"

Gram smiled, kissed him on the cheek, and said, "That's why we have raincoats!" Jimmy found a nice sandy area close to the fire to pitch his sleeping bag. The evening meal consisted of beef jerky and hardtack. Jimmy crawled into his sleeping bag and was fast asleep within seconds.

He woke up when Gram whispered, "Wake up, Jimmy. You need to wake up now."

He opened his eyes and asked, "Is it morning already?"

"No," said Gram. "Look over there." She was pointing to a glow coming from a short distance away.

"What is it?" asked Jimmy.

"Rustlers," answered Gram.

"Rustlers," screeched Jimmy. "Are they going to steal the cattle?"

"No, Jimmy," answered Gram. "We're going to stop them tonight."

Jimmy jumped up and asked, "How are we going to stop them?"

Gram smiled, winked, and replied, "Remember your training, Jimmy. That's how we'll stop them."

Jimmy winked back and said, "Oh yes, that's right. Let's go."

When Jimmy looked around, he noticed the others were dressed in black karate gi. He asked Gram why they were dressed like bad ninjas. Gram laughed and said, "That's a silly legend, Jimmy. A true ninja is always good. They wear white gi to show off their belt color and black gi to gain the element of surprise."

She handed him his black gi and said, "Get dressed. We leave in three minutes."

Jimmy put on his GI and said, "I'll saddle up."

"No horses, Jimmy. We're going on foot. We don't want them to know we're coming," replied Gram.

"I have already done reconnaissance and know the best way in," exclaimed Pete. "Follow me."

They hit a fast pace right off and didn't break stride until they were in the rustlers' camp. There were seven rustlers and seven of them. The rustlers jumped up and gave a good attempt at fighting back, but they didn't stand a chance. Within three minutes, not one rustler was left standing. Jimmy smiled and said, "This is one for the good guys!"

"Saddle up their horses. We'll ride them back to camp," shouted Pete. "They'll have a hard time rustling our cattle on foot." The sun came up just as they returned to camp, and it was time to saddle their own horses and start the cattle moving.

They had to hit the trail fast and hard to reach the grasslands before nightfall. It had plenty of grass and a creek. That meant both food and water for the cattle. The sun was still shining when they reached the grasslands, and the cattle went straight to the creek.

Everyone was exhausted, and Pete said, "Everybody sleeps tonight. Those cattle aren't going to leave this grass and water without being driven." Jimmy grabbed a piece of jerky and some hardtack, started chowing down while he was unsaddling his horse, and laid out his sleeping bag. He tossed his saddle down for a pillow, crawled in the sleeping bag, and fell asleep.

The camp came alive a little before sunrise, and this time, they got to eat breakfast before hitting the trail. Pete said, "We should reach the feed lot by four o'clock today and spend the night in a nice hotel room before we head back." Jimmy went over and sat down beside Gram.

He asked, "How come all these kids are ninjas like us?"

"Bullies have been around since the beginning of time," answered Gram. "Every kid your age that has been bullied has dreamed of ways to get even, your ancestors included."

Jimmy thought to himself, "We sure got even last night."

Suddenly, he realized all these kids were his ancestors. "Do they all know Mr. Jingles?" asked Jimmy.

"Yes," answered Gram. "And they will always be here for you anytime you ask for them."

That's so cool, thought Jimmy. He decided to learn more about each one of them on the way back to the bunkhouse.

Pete climbed on his horse and said, "Let's ride," and everyone followed. Jimmy had become a very confident rider and knew exactly what was expected of him, watching his portion of the herd and cutting back and bringing in that occasional stray.

It was around four o'clock when they reached their destination. When the last cow was delivered and the gate closed behind it, there was a general sigh of relief. The job was over and well done. Time to relax. They each got a room in the local hotel, showered, dressed, and met downstairs for a relaxing dinner.

Jimmy was seated with Martha, and he asked who she might be. "I'm Pete's Gram and very glad to meet you!" answered Martha.

"So are you a dreamer too?" asked Jimmy. "And have you known the magic of Mr. Jingles for a long time?"

"Oh yes," answered Martha. "Now, it's your turn. Why did you choose this adventure?" asked Martha. Jimmy got all excited and started telling her about his mare back home and how he needed to learn to ride.

Martha started laughing and said, "Sounds like you need to do more than learn to ride. You need to learn to communicate with your horse."

"How do you communicate with a horse?" asked Jimmy.

"So that's why Sara sat you next to me," replied Martha. "I'm not just a dreamer. I'm a horse whisperer as well."

"Can you teach me how to communicate with my horse?" asked Jimmy. Martha was pleased he asked for her help.

By the time they returned to the bunkhouse, Jimmy knew how to talk to his horse. They had reached the end of their journey, and this adventure was over. Jimmy had enjoyed the adventure but was anxious to see if he could talk to his horse. Gram took him by the hand and said, "Time to go home," and their descent began.

CHAPTER 4

SAVING THE FARM

When Jimmy woke up, it was morning and he was in his own bed. He didn't know how or when he got there, but the smell of bacon cooking told him how hungry he was. This time a shower could wait until after breakfast. Gram didn't disappoint him. A feast was waiting on the table. She told him to wash up and dig in.

After he finished eating and regained his strength, he asked, "Where do you get the strength to cook all this food, Gram? I can hardly get myself to the table."

"I have learned to adapt over the years," answered Gram. "Take a look in the refrigerator." Jimmy opened the refrigerator and started laughing. One whole shelf was filled with high-protein power shakes.

"Have you decided on a name for your horse?" asked Gram.

"I'm going to ask her today, but I'm pretty sure she'll agree on Sioux Z," replied Jimmy. They both shook their head in agreement, and Jimmy went upstairs to shower. He couldn't resist looking in the mirror to see if he had gained some more muscle. Sure enough, his arms and chest were a little bigger, and this time, he noticed his legs were getting more muscular.

He couldn't wait to see his horse, so he just yelled in passing to Gram, "I'll be back in a little while." When he opened the back door, there she was, standing at the gate, waiting for him. He started rubbing her neck and scratching behind her ears. He leaned in and whispered in her ear. She shook her head as if to say yes. "I knew it," said Jimmy. "I knew you would like the name Sioux Z."

He pulled a rope from around the fence post and made a hackamore for Sioux Z and slipped it over her head. He whispered again, and once more she shook her head. He jumped on her back, and they took off across the pasture. She was identical in every way to the Sioux Z on the cattle drive. Jimmy rode her for about an hour when he heard Gram calling.

She was standing on the first rung of the gate and reminded him that all the animals needed to be looked after. "All right," said Jimmy, "but can I ride Sioux Z and follow the tractor?"

"If that's what you want to do," answered Gram. "But I thought I would teach you to drive the tractor today."

"Okay. You talked me into it," responded Jimmy. "I'll drive the tractor now and ride Sioux Z some more when we get back."

"The horses should have enough hay left from that bale we took down the other day. We're going to take the smaller tractor with the front-end loader." Jimmy looked around, found a small John Deere tractor with a front-end loader, crawled, up and sat down.

"There's no room for you on this seat, Gram. Where are you going to ride?" asked Jimmy.

"I'll be seated on this tractor," replied Gram as she was getting on the tractor beside his.

"How are you going to teach me to drive over there?" asked Jimmy.

"They are geared the same, so just do what I do," answered Gram.

Jimmy watched closely as Gram pushed down on the brake pedal, turned the key to start the engine, and put the tractor in gear. She released the brake and pushed down on the gas pedal. The tractor started moving slowly toward the doors, so Jimmy did exactly the same thing and came in behind her.

He learned to use the controls to lower and raise the front-end loader when they stopped to fill it with grain. Gram was right: the horses had only eaten half the hay bale, so they dumped the grain in the feed trough and went to the creek. This time, Jimmy used the front-end loader to remove debris from the creek. They were finished a little before noon and headed back to the farmhouse.

They were laughing and having a good time when Gram looked up and noticed a big black car parked in the driveway. She motioned for Jimmy to look that way and told him to stick with her until they knew what was going on. A man in a uniform and cap got out of the front seat and opened the door for the man in the back. That man was dressed in a very expensive-looking pin-striped suit.

"That's far enough," said Gram. "What do you want?" The man introduced himself as Mark Wilson, land developer. He wanted to buy Gram's farm to build fancy condos and a new golf course. "My farm is not for sale," said Gram. "Now go away." Mark had a mean look on his face and said, "You're getting pretty old to live so far from town. You never know when some bad men might come and burn down your barn."

Jimmy had seen that look on Austin's face enough times to know when someone was being a bully. He stepped around Gram and exclaimed, "Gram said it isn't for sale, mister, so you'd best get on your way."

Mark turned to walk away and then stopped and retorted, "If bad things start happening, remember my offer." The two men got in that big black car and drove away.

"You know they'll be coming back again," cautioned Jimmy. "There's no telling what they'll do to force you into selling this place."

"Yes, and we'll be waiting for them," replied Gram. "It's just the two of us. We can't use Mr. Jingles's magic on this one, but we can use what we have learned." Jimmy just looked at Gram and said, "Let's get ready for them."

This meant a trip to town for supplies at the hardware store. All they needed was some motion detectors, night vision goggles, and a couple of electric fence wire boxes with plenty of wire. After they got back from town, they spent the rest of the day running a hot wire on top of the fencing to keep anyone from crawling over and sneaking up from the rear.

They set motion detectors across the front of the property to warn them if anyone was sneaking around. Jimmy knew what he had to do and was prepared to do it. Gram went in to start dinner, and Jimmy went to say "Good night" to Sioux Z. The sun looked like it was setting on the tree tops, and the clouds circling the sun were a brilliant red. *How beautiful*, thought Jimmy. *No wonder Gram won't sell.*

Jimmy went in for dinner and discussed strategy on what each of them could do to defend the place. Gram could fight with the best of them in her strong ten-year-old body, but not so much in this one. She went to the corner, picked up her baseball bat, and remarked, "You'd be surprised how hard I can swing this thing."

Jimmy laughed and said, "Well, I can fight, and I won't let anyone hurt you." She just smiled.

They knew they needed the element of surprise. The night vision goggles would give them an advantage the bad guys wouldn't be expecting. So would the motion detectors. "Let the bullies come," said Gram. "They just might get a lot more than they bargained for!"

They expected at least a couple of peaceful nights, and that was what they got. All the chores were done, and Sioux Z was broke and well trained. Gram and Jimmy should have been planning another adventure. However, for now, that wasn't going to happen.

They were sure there would be an unwelcomed visit by hired thugs, compliments of Mr. Mark Wilson, so they waited patiently. If Jimmy had learned anything from the master ninja, it was patience. They weren't worried, but they were prepared.

Day four was here, and absolutely nothing had happened. Jimmy wanted so bad to believe all was well and they could continue their adventures but something was nagging at him. Something was saying, "Stay put and wait. They are coming." So for now, he would have to be content riding Sioux Z, driving tractors, and swimming in the calf tank. When he thought about it, those were some really awesome things to do anyway.

They figured the trouble would come in the middle of the night when they were sleeping. Just to make sure nobody got the jump on them, Gram and Jimmy took turns standing guard at night. They didn't know who or how many would come, but it didn't matter. They were ready for anything. It was almost midnight on the fifth night, and Gram had just told Jimmy it was his turn to sleep, when one of the motion detectors went off.

There were no lights on in the house, so they put on the night vision goggles and went to check on who or what set it off. They were about to step outside when all the detectors started going off. Gram whispered, "They're here," and signaled that she was going out the front door as she picked up the bat.

Jimmy slipped out the back door and saw three men walking toward the barn. He could see them, but they couldn't see him. One man separated from the other two, so Jimmy took him out first with a kick to the head. He went after the other two, and without hesitation, he was hitting and kicking fast and hard.

A fourth man saw the commotion and came running, but Gram stepped out of the shadows and took him out with one swing of the bat. Four men came, and four went down. All four men were tied up, gagged, and put in the back of Gram's truck, to be escorted to town.

Gram parked in front of the offices of Mark Wilson, land developer. She told Jimmy to keep an eye on those thugs, and she went in. She marched right past the secretary and entered an office that had "Mark Wilson" written on the door. She blurted out, "I believe I have something that belongs to you outside. Come and get them or I'll take them to the sheriff." The look on Mark's face was of total shock when he saw those four men tied up.

"That's right, Mr. Wilson," said Gram. "My barn is still standing and my land is still mine. Find somewhere else to build your fancy condos and golf course." Jimmy started dragging the men out of the truck, dropping them on the ground. Gram and Jimmy got back in the truck and drove off.

Jimmy asked Gram if she was going to report them to the sheriff, and she said, "It won't do any good. Besides, this isn't over. He will send more next time. We need to pick up a few more supplies." This time they stopped at the feed store and picked up outdoor cameras, rope, and some fishing nets.

When they got home, Gram said, "Let's get some sleep. They won't be back tonight." Jimmy was OK with that, but he wanted to visit Sioux Z first. As usual, she was waiting at the gate for him and whinnied when she saw him coming. He was tired but figured a thirty-minute ride with his best friend would be all right. He slipped the hackamore over her head, jumped on her back, and said, "Take me anywhere you want to go."

Sioux Z made a beeline for the gate at the back fence. There was a pretty little buckskin mare waiting for them on the other side of the fence. "Well," said Jimmy. "What do we have here?" Sioux Z went over to the gate latch and started nudging it with her nose. "You want me to open the gate and let her in?" asked Jimmy. Sioux Z nodded her head in approval, so Jimmy said, "All right," and opened the gate. The buckskin trotted through the gate and nudged Jimmy with her nose. "You're welcome," said Jimmy and he started laughing.

He could break this mare for Gram so they could ride together. He kissed Sioux Z on the nose and said, "Thanks, what a great idea." Jimmy remounted, and they headed to the barn. The buckskin stayed right on their tail until they came to a stop. He put out enough grain for two horses and said "Good night."

Gram had already gone to bed, so Jimmy was very quiet when he went into the house. He decided to not tell her about the buckskin but surprise her with it later. First at hand was getting rid of Mark Wilson. Jimmy was very confident they would defeat this man. Especially since he discovered the things he learns in Mr. Jingles's world, works in the real world.

Early the next morning, Gram and Jimmy went out to set traps. Gram went to the barn and brought out the backhoe. She dug two holes, ten feet deep, about twenty feet apart. She stretched a fake trip wire between the two holes, raising it high enough that an intruder would see it. The holes were covered with thin plywood, dirt, and weeds. The intruders should see the trip wire, go around it, and hopefully, fall into one of the ten-foot holes.

A couple of feet from the outside of both deep pit holes, Gram laid the fish nets flat on the ground. She used a come-along to lower a tree branch about eight feet. Jimmy tied ropes to all four corners of the net while Gram secured the other end of the four ropes to a single rope.

She had Jimmy climb out on the branch, and she tossed him the single rope. After he secured it to the branch, Gram tossed him a black rope to tie around the branch. She tied the other end of the black rope to a snare-trap trigger. When Gram released the come-along, the trap was set. The slightest touch on the trigger would send a perpetrator eight feet in the air.

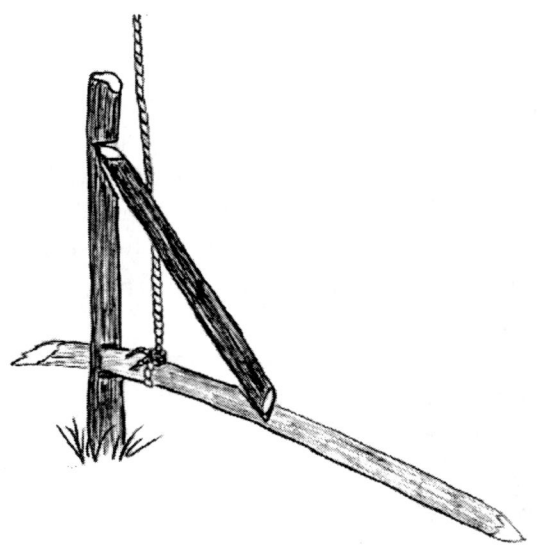

After the snare traps were finished, Gram had Jimmy dig ten holes two feet deep with a posthole digger. She took a spade shovel and dug out the top of the holes, about twenty-four inches around, approximately one foot deep. After cutting ten boards twenty-four inches long, Jimmy marked the center of each board and sawed them halfway through to weaken the board. He hammered eight nails at a forty-five-degree angle on each side of every board.

After placing a board in each hole with nails pointed up, they put twigs over the top of the holes to hide them. If a person stepped on the twigs, their leg would fall in the hole and break the board, driving the nails against the leg. If they tried to get out, the nails would get tighter on the leg.

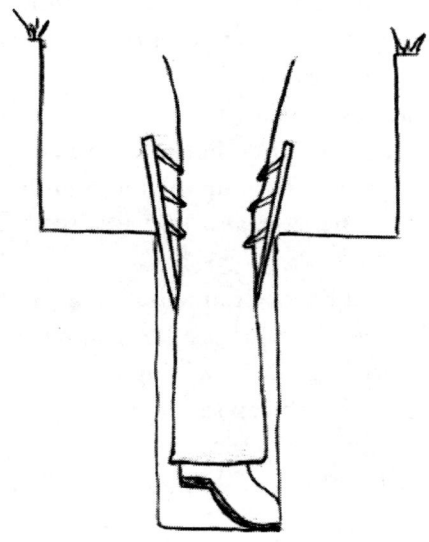

Last, but not least, were the cameras. These would be placed in the least expected yet the most strategic places possible. They would be hidden in birdhouses and behind tree limbs, where nobody would expect a camera to be. Four cameras were put up, covering all possible entrances onto the property. The cameras were wired into a single television in the house that monitored all four views at one time.

"I don't know how many men Mark will send," said Gram, "but the traps should get most of them."

"Don't worry," replied Jimmy. "I can handle anyone that makes it past the traps."

"We can handle them," said Gram. "We're a team. Regardless of my age, you and I will do this together.

"But for now, you have a friend in the pasture in need of some tender loving care. Go take care of her!"

"You're the best," said Jimmy. "Just keep your bat close at hand." Jimmy was out the door, headed for the pasture. He had two friends waiting for him, and he couldn't wait to start riding the buckskin.

He made a new hackamore halter for the buckskin and slipped it over her head. He whispered, oh so softly in her ear, "We can do this, pretty girl. You and I are going to run like the wind." She nodded her head in approval, and Jimmy jumped on her back. He leaned forward and gently kicked her in the sides.

They took off across the pasture like they had been shot out of a cannon. Sioux Z was right on their heels. They were running, jumping, kicking, and enjoying the cool hours of the evening. Jimmy was sure this was a little piece of heaven, and that was why Gram would fight to keep it.

Two more days went by without incident, and both Gram and Jimmy wanted to believe their private life could go on without interruption. They were not, however, willing to take a chance. Instead, they waited, once again, for the ax to fall.

On the fourth night, the motion detectors went crazy. The alarms sent both Gram and Jimmy scrambling downstairs, hoping to get an idea of what was pending. They watched the cameras to get an idea of how many intruders came and how many would be captured in the traps.

They watched as their enemy found the trip wire and split into two groups to go around it. There were ten in all; five went to the right, and five went to the left. The timing was perfect, and both deep pit traps went off at the same time, trapping three men.

The seven remaining proceeded around the holes, stepping cautiously. They were expecting more holes, but not snare traps. The one on the left went first, capturing two more men, and then the one on the right scooped up one more. "Six down and four to go," said Jimmy. "I'm going outside to wait for them in case any get through the next traps."

The ten leg traps captured two more, leaving two for Jimmy to deal with. He waited in the shadows, out of sight, while the enemy came to him. The two culprits left were busy looking for more traps, giving Jimmy the upper hand with the element of surprise.

When they passed his position, a foot came up striking one of them in the face, and two more very fast kicks to the head knocked that one out. The last man turned to run away and stepped on a rake. The prongs were sticking up, causing the handle to fly up, striking the man in the face, knocking him out.

Jimmy was still laughing when Gram got there. "What's so funny?" she asked.

Jimmy pointed at the rake and said, "That wasn't a trap. I just forgot to put it away." They both had a good laugh and then started the task of tying up the bad guys and putting them in the back of Gram's truck.

Once again, Gram and Jimmy headed into town with a truckload of Mark's hired thugs. Gram was laying on the horn when she pulled up at the land developer's office. "Mr. Wilson!" she yelled. "Come get your trash!" Mark stepped out of his office, shaking his head in disapproval as his men were being thrown on the ground.

"This ends now!" shouted Gram. "Come at us again and we'll be coming after you."

Mark was still shaking his head when he looked at Gram and remarked, "I withdraw my offer to purchase your land. The mayor wants us to build closer to town anyway, so have a nice life."

A defeated Mark Wilson disappeared into his office while Gram and Jimmy drove away smiling. "That was so cool," said Jimmy. "This time the bully lost!" They spent the rest of the day getting rid of traps and laughing every time they looked at that silly rake.

After dinner, Gram said they could take off on another adventure right after breakfast. Jimmy was excited, but not about the new adventure. He asked if they could spend one more day at home. He had a surprise for her and couldn't wait another day for her to see it.

"OK," said Gram with a surprised look on her face. "If that's what you want."

"I have to go see Sioux Z," replied Jimmy as he headed out the door.

Gram just giggled, shrugged her shoulders, and said, "Kids."

The next morning, right after breakfast, Jimmy asked Gram to go with him to the pasture. He was so excited it made Gram even more curious about her surprise, so she said, "Let's go." She couldn't believe her eyes when she saw the buckskin mare.

"Is she for me?" asked Gram.

"She sure is," answered Jimmy. "Do you like her?" Tears formed in Gram's eyes as she leaned over and kissed Jimmy on the cheek.

"What made you think of doing this for me?" she asked.

"It wasn't my idea," confessed Jimmy. "It was Sioux Z's." So Gram bent over and kissed Sioux Z on the nose, and they both laughed.

They saddled up the horses and took off across the pasture following the fence row. Gram told Jimmy this would be a perfect time for him to get a good layout of the land. They rode down the bluff, across the lower pasture, and through the creek to the other side.

They continued over more pasture until they finally came to another tree line. Gram pointed to the trees and said, "There's a hundred acres of trees here. It's full of wildlife. The fence that marks the end of our property is behind those trees."

"It's so beautiful, Gram. I love it," replied Jimmy.

"Good," said Gram. "I've hired an attorney to have your name added to everything here in case something happens to me."

"Nothing's going to happen to you. I won't let it," answered Jimmy. She smiled and told him how she had told Gramps the same thing a long time ago.

She reminisced about the many wonderful adventures they had together while he prepared her to take over. "Now, I'm preparing you to take over for me someday," explained Gram. "But, not today. We have another adventure in the morning." She took off yelling, "Race you home!" and the race was on.

Jimmy made sure everything outside was locked down, fed, and watered while Gram took care of everything in the house, including a big dinner. They enjoyed a good conversation over dinner, pondering the events of the last few days. The best part of the conversation was laughing at the idiot that knocked himself out with the rake.

Jimmy smiled and thought to himself, "Sure glad that wasn't me. He'll never live that one down." They finished their conversation with dessert eaten outside. Gram had made a fresh peach cobbler, and Jimmy wasn't going to let it go to waste. After dessert, Jimmy gave Gram a big hug and said, "Good night."

CHAPTER 5

THE DRAGON SLAYER

Early the next morning, Jimmy was up, showered, and ready to get started on the next adventure. He flew down the stairs and rounded the corner, expecting to see Gram. The food was on the table, but no Gram. "That's odd," he thought as he started looking all around for her.

He found her at the pasture gate handing grain to the buckskin mare. "Have you thought of a name for her?" he asked.

"Not yet, but I'll think of something before we get back," answered Gram. They went inside to eat breakfast and begin their next adventure.

Breakfast was finished and dishes cleaned and put away. Jimmy was holding Mr. Jingles in one hand and reaching out to Gram with the other as he said, "Time to go." She didn't even ask where they were going this time. After all, it was his adventure, and she was quickly learning to trust his imagination.

With this in mind, she took his hand and closed her eyes, and they were off again. They landed outside a moat that surrounded and protected a castle. "Medieval times," said Gram. "Good choice." Jimmy was even more impressed with Mr. Jingles when he discovered his and Gram's attire changed en route. It was a good thing because they would have stuck out like a sore thumb in blue jeans and T-shirts.

The moat bridge was already down, making entry to the castle easy. All they had to do was walk across the bridge, and nobody even seemed to notice. Once inside, they discovered why it was so easy to get in. It seemed the entire countryside was being terrorized by an uncontrollable dragon. The people were coming to the castle for protection.

Jimmy looked at Gram and said, "I guess there are bullies in every land and every species."

He got a funny look on his face and asked, "Are we going to be able to help these people?"

"Yes," said Gram, "but we're going to need help. They found an empty room where nobody could see them, and Gram showed Jimmy how to summon his ancestors.

This time, six kids came—the five that were on the cattle drive and one more. Gram said, "Meet Edgar. He was a famous wizard and magician." Jimmy shook Edgar's hand and asked if wizards were experts on slaying dragons.

"That's certainly my specialty," said Edgar. "That's why Mr. Jingles sent me. Learn to trust him. He will always give you exactly what you need."

Edgar told everyone to split up in groups of two and find out as much as they could about this dragon. He told them to be back with the information in three hours. Jimmy wasn't sure how to know when three hours were up because there were no clocks around. He figured he'd leave that to Mr. Jingles.

He and Gram walked around listening to every conversation about the dragon. People had different ideas about ways to get rid of it. They managed to strike up a conversation with a woman claiming to be a survivor of a dragon attack. She said it was a three-headed dragon and all three heads breathed fire.

They overheard a man say the dragon lived about fifty miles to the east in a volcano. Some people thought it would take an army to kill the dragon, while others believed it would only take one. They walked around the castle and found themselves right back where they were supposed to meet Edgar. All of the others arrived at exactly the same time.

Edgar was waiting for them inside. He was holding a strange-looking tablet, a big, round, clear-looking ball, and a stick with fire coming out one end. When everyone started telling what they had learned, Edgar used the stick to write notes on the tablet. After everybody stopped talking, Edgar said, "Give me a minute to figure this out."

He set the tablet on a table beside the clear ball and started circling his hands over the top of it. The words looked like fire as they started following the rotation of Edgar's hands. His hands stopped moving, and he started pulling the words off the tablet and smearing them on the outside of the clear ball. When the last word was taken from the tablet, Edgar's hand came up, and he threw it at the ball. There was a bright flash of light, and all the words were inside the ball, still circling.

"The ball will tell us how to slay the dragon and stay alive," said Edgar. He seemed to be in a trance and was speaking in a very mellow tone. "The dragon has three heads but only one brain. The only way to kill it is to cut off the head that holds the brain. If the wrong head is removed, fire will shoot out of the neck, killing the one holding the sword. The dragon will grow a new head and continue to live. Approach the dragon with caution. All three heads breathe fire.

"The best place to sneak up on the dragon is where it sleeps. This place can be found in the center of an active volcano, east of the castle. There is a large opening at the front of the volcano. Many have gone in and none have come out. On the back side of the volcano, halfway up, is a small opening. It is big enough to pass through and the only safe entrance. The dragon always sleeps facing the large opening with one head watching in that direction at all times.

"Before getting to the dragon, one will be tested three times. The first test is compassion, the second is loyalty, and the third is courage. One must possess all three to gain safe passage. This passage is a direct route to the main chamber and the resting place of the dragon. Before the dragon can be killed, one must know the answer to this riddle.

A dragon with three heads
Is a sight to see!
But looking is as dangerous
As dangerous can be.
To kill the dragon
You cut off his head
Cut off the wrong one
And you will be dead.
To find the right one
You must solve this riddle.
Which one do you cut?
It's the one __ __ __

That was the end of the information, and the clear ball went blank. Edgar's mind returned from wherever it had been, and the room went silent. Generation after generation had been on these adventures, but they had never encountered anything like this.

"Time for a family meeting," said Gram. She explained how the family always stuck together and not one time before had just one member fought alone.

Jimmy stepped up and said, "It's all right, Gram. I can do this!"

Gram put her hands on both sides of Jimmy's face, looked him in the eyes, and said, "I can't lose you, Jimmy. Are you sure?"

"I can do this. Please trust me," said Jimmy. "I won't let you down. I promise."

Gram hugged him with all her might and said, "All right, but I'm going with you and it's not up for debate."

Jimmy chuckled and said, "I thought you'd say that. Let's do this!" Gram and Jimmy told the others good-bye and started looking around the castle for the supplies they would need to kill the dragon.

Gram said, "We will need helmets, shields, and swords. We need to find the blacksmith."

The blacksmith agreed to build the supplies for three pieces of gold. "I don't have any gold," said Jimmy. Gram rolled her eyes and said, "Look in your pocket. I told you, Mr. Jingles always provides." He reached in his pocket and pulled out three pieces of gold. "Oh yes," said Jimmy. "I forgot! It's magic."

The blacksmith measured them both and got busy with the task. They agreed to return in two hours for their gear and set out to find a donkey and saddlebags to carry their supplies. Once they collected everything they needed, they left the castle and crossed the moat bridge.

Waiting on the other side was the rest of the family on horseback and two extra horses. Edgar smiled and said, "You didn't really think you were going to make the entire journey alone, did you?" Gram was just shaking her head when Edgar said, "We have to wait until dark before we start the journey. The dragon flies in the daylight and sleeps at night. Let's not let him know we're coming."

Gram stopped shaking her head, smiled, and said, "OK, we need you." They all started laughing, and Edgar said, "Besides, who's going to teach you how to use those swords? They are different from ninja swords." They got busy setting up camouflage netting. They would wait under the netting until sundown.

It was very dark when they took down the netting and started their journey. Pete rode beside Jimmy and started teaching him how to use the stars to find his way at night. He told Jimmy that regardless of where you were on earth, the stars remained constant. If you learned the patterns of all the star constellations and knew their location, they would tell you the direction you were traveling. They rode all night, and Jimmy memorized every constellation in the sky.

At the first sign of light, they set the netting back up to conceal their whereabouts. Gram and Jimmy started lessons on using the new swords while the others plotted their course. They figured it would take two nights of hard riding to arrive at their destination.

They would spend one more day under the netting and enter the cave after dark. They left at nightfall and arrived on the back side of the volcano in perfect time. They used the day to rest up and unpack the gear they would be taking with them. Jimmy contemplated different scenarios on how he would handle the dragon.

He went over the words Edgar had pulled from the clear ball and started repeating them over and over in his head. *I'll be tested three times.* He figured he would be okay with the tests. He knew he was compassionate and loyal, and thanks to Mr. Jingles, he had become courageous as well.

His thoughts went back to the riddle, and he repeated it again. He started doubting himself and asked Gram, "What if I can't solve the riddle?"

"This is your dream, your imagination, your adventure, and you can control it," answered Gram. She continued by saying, "Mr. Jingles would not have put you here if he didn't trust you. Now you must trust in Mr. Jingles and his magic."

They were starting up the volcano wall as the sun was setting. The dragon would be asleep by the time they reached the cave. They used the moonlight to find the cave opening but took the torches from their bag before entering the cave.

Not too far into the cave, Jimmy spotted a small white mouse on a rock. "What are you doing in this old dark cave?" asked Jimmy. He looked up and saw a snake slithering toward the mouse. He picked up the mouse and put it in his pocket to keep it safe.

As they proceeded deeper into the cave, a vine grabbed Gram by the leg and pulled her down. It was retracting into a hole between some rocks, pulling Gram with it. Jimmy grabbed her and tried pulling her away, but couldn't break her loose. More vines started coming out of the rocks, and Gram said, "Run, Jimmy, save yourself."

Jimmy answered, "No way!" pulled out his sword, and started slicing vines. They turned Gram loose and retreated back into the rocks.

"Thanks," said Gram. "I thought I was a goner."

"We go together or we don't go at all," said Jimmy. He looked at Mr. Jingles and said, "Thank you," and Mr. Jingles started glowing. That glow took away all of Jimmy's anxieties. He asked Gram if she was ready to continue, and she nodded yes. They were stepping much more carefully, watching in every direction.

They were almost to the dragon's habitat when a troll stepped out from behind a boulder and demanded they stop. The troll said, "No, no, no, you cannot go. You don't pass the troll 'til you pay the toll."

"What's the toll?" asked Jimmy.

"Give me the girl and you can pass," answered the troll.

"I don't think so," said Jimmy as he jumped in the air and gave the troll a side thrust kick to the head. The troll went flying backward and landed flat on his back. Jimmy put his sword to the troll's neck and said, "Can we pass now?"

The troll snarled and said, "Go."

They passed the troll and went on their way. Jimmy stopped, looked at Gram, and said, "The troll was courage, the vines were loyalty, but what was the compassion?"

Gram started laughing and said, "I think it's the mouse in your pocket!"

He had forgotten all about that little fellow, so he reached in his pocket and took him out. The mouse was twitching his nose and looking so cute. Jimmy said, "I think you will be safer here." He gently set him on a rock and patted him on the head, and the mouse ran away.

They finally reached the edge of the room where the dragon slept. There it was, all curled up with two heads sleeping and one head watching the main entrance to its domain. Jimmy motioned for Gram to stay put while he went in. He was circling, clinging to the walls for cover.

The walls were cold and creepy. However, the moonlight shining through the large front cave opening created shadows for Jimmy to hide in. He would slither from one shadow to another. If he wanted to keep the element of surprise, he would have to remain as quiet as the little mouse he had been holding in his pocket.

He was repeating the riddle over and over in his mind. He knew he needed to figure out which head to chop off before confronting the dragon. All of a sudden, the dragon head standing guard spotted him. It let out an ear-piercing scream and woke the other two heads.

The fight was on, and each head would take a turn biting at Jimmy and breathing fire at him. The shield protected him from the bites and the fire. He said the riddle one last time. "To find the right head, I must solve the riddle. Which one should I cut? It's the one *in the middle*."

With those words in his head, he slashed with his sword, and off went the dragon's middle head. The dragon fell to the ground, and Jimmy gave a big sigh of relief. Gram started jumping up and down, dancing for joy. Once again, he looked at Mr. Jingles and said, "Thank you." He was sure Mr. Jingles winked at him.

They were picking up a few dragon scales to give to the townspeople when Jimmy heard a cooing sound. He started looking around, and to his surprise, it was a baby dragon, not much bigger than a kitten. "Look, Gram," said Jimmy. "It's a baby! What shall we do with it?"

Gram shrugged her shoulders and said, "I don't know. Let's take it with us and ask Edgar."

They finished their task, and the three of them started out of the cave. The family was waiting anxiously for their arrival at the mouth of the cave. Finally, they appeared, and cheers roared to the heavens. They had killed the dragon, and the countryside was safe. Hugs were passed around, and they were all patting Jimmy on the back.

Jimmy suddenly remembered the baby in his backpack. He pulled it out and handed it to Edgar. "What in the world can we do with this?" he asked.

"You can present this perfect little specimen to the king's wizard," replied Edgar. "He will know what to do with it."

The return trip to the castle was much faster and pleasant since the dragon was no longer a threat. They could ride in the daylight hours and enjoy the scenery. With the threat gone, the family's mood changed from serious to playful. Everyone was joking around and having a good time.

Gram rode up beside Jimmy to congratulate him on a job well done. "Thanks," he said. "But I'm curious. Why do you suppose nobody ever told me there had been a wizard in the family?"

Gram answered with a question. "How much did you know about me?"

Jimmy's answer was simple. "Nothing. I didn't even know I had a grandmother."

Gram went on to explain how they have a special gift and how family members without the gift don't understand. They especially didn't understand Edgar. Not only was he a dreamer; he could also do things that defied all logic. Instead of embracing his magic, they were frightened by it.

Then she said, "Most of us with the gift think it was Edgar that conjured up Mr. Jingles. He has never admitted it, so we really don't know for sure."

"Really?" said Jimmy. "Has anyone ever asked him?"

"If he wanted us to know, he would have told us," said Gram. "All that really matters is that we have the gift of Mr. Jingles."

The news about the slain dragon beat them to the castle, and cheering could be heard for miles. The king ordered a feast in honor of the dragon slayer, and Jimmy presented the baby dragon to the wizard. The wizard told Jimmy he would train the baby to defend the country-side from rogue dragons that threatened the people. The king gave the order to name the baby dragon Jimmy the Great.

Jimmy graciously accepted the honor, and this adventure was over.

CHAPTER 6

RUNNING WITH THE LIONS

Jimmy's eyes opened with the sun shining bright and the smell of biscuits and bacon. He rolled out of bed, and the only thing he wanted to do was eat. He knew what was waiting for him in the kitchen, and he headed that way. He heard Gram say "Good morning" as he opened the kitchen door.

Jimmy couldn't wait to see Sioux Z and tell her all about slaying a dragon, but he wanted to take a little time to talk to Gram before he went out to start chores. Jimmy asked, "Have you thought of a name for your mare?"

"Sure have!" answered Gram. "I believe I'll name her Dragon Slayer and call her Dragon for short."

He nodded in agreement and asked if he could take the tractor down the bluff to check the creek. She wanted to be with him but knew he had to strike out on his own sooner or later. Besides, she would be no more than ten minutes behind him with a bale of hay anyway.

Jimmy spent a little time taking hay and grain to Sioux Z and Dragon before taking the tractor out of the barn. He was overjoyed that Gram trusted him with a tractor. He knew, within reason, that there was no way he would disappoint her. He carefully picked up a load of grain and headed across the pasture to the bluffs.

He was careful to follow the path Gram took because he knew it was safe. Once he was in the pasture, he dropped the grain in the feeder and started toward the creek. About half way to the creek, he noticed something black lying down in the tall grass.

He knew there was work to be done, but his curiosity got the better of him. He turned the tractor in that direction so he could get a better look. As he got closer, he realized it was a newborn calf. He looked around for its mother but didn't see any other cows at all. He got off the tractor to make sure the calf was alive, and sure enough, it was very much alive.

He saw Gram coming down the bluff, so he picked up the calf and carried it to his tractor. Work or no work, something had to be done about this baby, so he went to meet Gram. She dropped the bale of hay she had brought to the horses and told Jimmy that he and the calf could ride with her to the barn.

They needed to get the veterinarian out to check the calf while they went to find its mother. After the veterinarian arrived, Gram and Jimmy saddled up the horses and set out to search. They split up so they could cover more ground. They did, however, stay within calling distance just in case one of them found something.

Jimmy came across a heifer with a newborn calf beside her. It looked identical to the one he found earlier, so he called out for Gram. "Looks like she had twins and wandered off before the second calf was strong enough to follow," said Gram. Jimmy got on one side of the calf and heifer, Gram got on the other side, and they started driving them toward the barn.

When they reached the barn, the vet opened the barn door and told Gram the abandoned calf was fine. They were put into a small pen, but the mother wanted nothing to do with the calf she had abandoned. "What can we do?" asked Jimmy.

"We won't give her a choice," replied Gram. They ran the heifer into a squeeze chute and closed the sides down tight until she couldn't move.

Gram started milking her, squirting milk at first one baby then another. Everyone got a good laugh watching those babies licking the milk off their faces. It wasn't long until the babies were full and the heifer was released into the pen with her babies for the night.

"If she's not feeding both babies by morning, we'll do it again," remarked Gram. Gram told Jimmy to make sure the heifer had plenty of hay and water while she went to fix dinner. After dinner, they went outside and sat on the front porch to enjoy the evening and have dessert.

Gram had cookies and coffee, while Jimmy had cookies and milk. They talked about the events of the day, the events of past adventures, and the next adventure to come. Jimmy thought to himself, *I've been here almost a month and haven't turned on a television or a game!"* He smiled at Gram and said, "Good night."

After a good night's sleep, Jimmy woke up refreshed and ready to start another day. He got dressed and hurried outside to check on the heifer. He swung open the barn doors and turned on the light. There she was, eating hay, and both calves were nursing. The only problem now was telling one calf from another.

They were identical, and both seemed to be very healthy. Gram walked up behind Jimmy and whispered, "We'll give them a couple of days in the barn before we put them back in the pasture." That was fine with Jimmy. He had never seen a newborn calf. He wanted to pet them, but he figured it wasn't a good idea to spook the mom.

The chores didn't get done the day before, so that meant double chores today. Jimmy didn't care since he'd get to drive the tractor again. He was having so much fun. He was sure things couldn't get any better. Then Gram told him he could have the heifer and twin calves to start his own herd. "That is so awesome!" said Jimmy. "Thanks."

All he had to do now was put a tag in their ear with his name on it so he could identify them later. Gram let him know that just like Sioux Z, the cows were also his responsibility, and he had to take care of them. He liked the idea of being needed and feeling useful. He wasn't sure how he would take care of his animals when he had to return home but figured on facing that when the time came.

Actually, he hoped that time would never come. This was the happiest he had ever been and was sure this was where he belonged. "Well, at least I'm here for now and have some work to do," thought Jimmy. He hoped to finish his chores in time to ride Sioux Z before dinner.

After making sure the animals at the house had plenty of food and water, he jumped on the tractor and took off across the pasture as happy as a Lark. He kept looking back, wondering if Gram was going to follow him. He wasn't sure since she had taken the hay down the day before.

When he got to the tree line, there was still no sign of her, and he was getting a little worried. When he got to really thinking about it, he hadn't seen her since early that morning in the barn. He figured he would finish checking the creek as quickly as possible and hurry back to check on Gram.

He followed the usual path through the trees and down the bluff. He checked the grain and hay then continued toward the creek. When the creek drew near, he saw a horse that looked just like Dragon. His curiosity made him speed up a little, and soon it became clear that Gram wasn't following him because she was already there. He was relieved to know she was all right and delighted to see she brought lunch.

She had laid out a blanket and brought a basket filled with Jimmy's favorite foods. "What a great idea!" said Jimmy.

"Thanks, but it wasn't my idea," replied Gram. "It was Dragon's. She thought you could use the nourishment."

It seemed they could always find something to talk about, and Jimmy never got bored or lost interest in their conversations. He figured it was because they were so much alike and shared the same wonderful family secret.

An hour passed, and lunchtime was over. Jimmy went back to work, and Gram packed up to go home. There was plenty of work to be done before they could start a new adventure, and they both looked forward to that.

Later that evening, Gram asked Jimmy if he had decided where he wanted the next adventure to take them. "I haven't got a clue," said Jimmy. "What if I can't think of something?"

Gram laughed, told him not to worry, and whispered in his ear, "Just let Mr. Jingles decide. He always knows best anyway."

Two more days had come and gone. All of the chores were done, and the heifer was feeding both calves without a problem. It was time to saddle up and drive them back to the pasture. Driving cattle might be work for some people, but Jimmy was thinking it was just plain fun. They reached the pasture by midmorning, and the heifer started grazing while the calves started suckling.

"Race you back," said Gram.

"You're on," replied Jimmy. And they were off.

They raced up the bluff, through the trees, and across the pasture, with their horses staying nose to nose. They reached the gate at the same time and were both laughing. They dismounted and walked their horses the rest of the way to cool them down.

Jimmy told Gram he would take the horses to the barn and brush them before he came in. With that being said, Gram went in the house to start dinner. When Jimmy finished outside, he went in the house. Gram was standing by the counter, holding the phone in her hand. "It's your father. He wants to talk to you," said Gram as she handed him the phone.

Jimmy took the phone and started telling his dad about the ranch, how much fun he was having, and all the cool things he was learning to do. The more he talked, the more excited he became. He couldn't thank his dad enough for sending him to stay with Gram.

He got very quiet for a minute, then Gram heard him say, "No, Dad. You said I would be here for the whole summer, and I don't want to come home." He continued by saying Gram would get him a ticket a couple of days before school starts.

Gram was getting worried and shook her head yes at Jimmy. She smiled when she heard him say, "OK. I'll see you in a couple of months." She hung up the phone as Jimmy said, "Wow, that was close."

Jimmy washed up and sat down to eat. "Have you figured out where you want to go yet?" asked Gram.

"No," answered Jimmy. "I think I'll let Mr. Jingles decide."

"I sure hope it doesn't include horse racing," said Gram as she reminded him how he let an old woman keep up with him. He quickly reminded her that she was old only part of the time, so it didn't count.

Laughter was heard around the house as the two of them enjoyed the evening just being together. They were really looking forward to a new adventure in the morning. But that was tomorrow. They had this evening to reminisce about some of their last adventures.

Morning came, breakfast was over, and they were ready to go. They drifted off and waited to see where they would end up. When they touched down and their eyes opened, Jimmy looked around and asked, "Where are we?"

"In Africa," said Gram. Neither of them new why but figured it wouldn't take long to find out.

All of a sudden, they heard the loud cry of a lion. This wasn't a vicious cry but instead a desperate cry for help. Jimmy started walking in the direction the cries were coming from. "Careful!" said Gram. "It is a lion."

"I know, but something's wrong. I need to find out what it is," replied Jimmy.

The closer they got, the louder and more desperate the cry became. They found themselves in an opening. They had come face-to-face with the lioness. Jimmy started talking to her as he walked in her direction.

They stood face-to-face, whispering to each other, until Jimmy turned to Gram and said, "This is Shayla, and she has lost her cub and needs help finding him."

He reassured Shayla and promised to help find her baby. As the lioness told Jimmy what had happened, he relayed the information to Gram.

Some men came with guns, cages, and nets to capture animals. She told her cub, Sengemo, to run and hide. She taunted the men to follow her and thought Sengemo was safe. When she was sure the men lost her trail, she doubled back to get him, but he was gone.

Jimmy asked if she thought the men might have captured Sengemo, and the lioness just lowered her head and cried. Jimmy and Gram started looking around, finding lots of boot prints, and figured out the direction the poachers were traveling. He told Shayla they would find the men and set all the animals free, but they would need her help.

"I will do anything you ask of me," said Shayla.

"Good," replied Jimmy. "You do your hunting at night and can navigate the jungle in the dark. That's what we need you to do. Those men can only see in the daylight and must camp when it gets dark. With you leading us at night, we won't stop moving until we find them."

"Let me have Mr. Jingles," said Gram. "We need an expert tracker, and that would be Daniel. He can track a needle through a haystack." Gram took Mr. Jingles and requested Daniel's presence. As soon as he arrived, they were ready to find Sengemo. Daniel set a fairly rapid pace, stopping only when the footprints changed direction.

After a couple of hours on the trail, they came upon two more lionesses. Shayla told Jimmy they were her sisters Bayhas and Lea. They were from the same pride as she and also lost their babies. Bayhas and Lea agreed to join the quest to free all the animals. Daniel reset the pace and tracked until nightfall when Shayla took the lead.

The next day, they were joined by Lubaya and Shange, two more lionesses from Shayla's pride. They also had missing cubs. They were very happy to learn that a rescue mission was in progress. Daniel told them he was sure they were gaining on the poachers. "It shouldn't be long now," he said.

The poachers didn't appear to be getting anywhere. Their tracks would turn right, then left, and right again. Daniel held up his hand, turned to Gram, and laughingly said, "These foolish poachers have gotten themselves lost."

They decided to rest while Daniel checked it out. He told the others he wouldn't be long, and he left the camp. All the zigzagging the poachers were doing was slowing them down, and Daniel returned in a few minutes. He was laughing and said, "They are only a couple hundred yards ahead of us and not moving."

The plan was to stay put and rest until dark. When the poachers started a campfire for the night, it would be a dead giveaway to their location. Daniel would continue to do reconnaissance and keep the others informed. He would let them know when it was time to advance on the poachers.

Daniel said, "First we need to decide what we want to do about the poachers before we hit their camp. If we release the animals and leave the poachers to the mercy of the jungle, they will surely die!"

Jimmy just sat thinking for a couple of minutes before answering. "The poachers are the bullies of the jungle, and they definitely need to be taught a lesson in humility," he said.

He thought about it a couple more minutes and said, "We will capture the poachers, release the animals, and take the poachers out of the jungle locked in their own cages." It was agreed by all that this was a perfect plan. Even the lions were happy with it.

Gram put her hand on Jimmy's shoulder and said, "The ninja master would be very proud of you right now."

It was decided that the lions would subdue the poachers while Jimmy, Gram, and Daniel released the animals. Once the animals were freed, the lions would drive the poachers into the cages. If all went as planned, the only injury would be to the poachers' wounded pride. That is, if everything went as planned. If not, they could handle that too. They may, however, need to wound more than just the poachers' pride.

It would be very dark by the time they started toward the poachers' camp. Even though they would be able to see the glow from the poachers' campfire, the lions would still need to lead the others through the dense foliage of the jungle. The lions gave the rescuers the advantage. They weren't just nocturnal animals; they were also mothers on a quest to save their children.

It was very late when Daniel came back to camp and said, "It's time." He told the lions to surround the camp, and when he made the sound of the singing bush lark, they would pounce in unison. The lions were so eager to see their cubs; when Daniel said go, the pace was set at a run with the lions leading. Jimmy, Gram, and Daniel were bringing up the rear and had no trouble keeping up.

When they arrived at the camp, the lions took their position and waited for Daniel to make the call. When the call sounded, the lions pounced on the sleeping poachers, pinning them to the ground. There were six poachers, so Shayla pinned two men. She hoped they would attempt to escape, giving her a reason to stop them. They, however, just trembled in fear as Shayla's teeth glistened in the moonlight.

Jimmy and the others rushed in and started opening cages. They released mandrills, baboons, macaques, African black pythons, and other snakes, including the black mamba. There were also baby crocodiles, leopards, cheetahs, the African wild dog also known as the cape hunting dog, and a lesser bush baby. There were many other birds and animals, including a very rare red colobus monkey.

Once the cages were emptied, the lions roared and drove the poachers into the cages. Jimmy closed the doors and fastened the locks. He didn't understand why the babies didn't run away. They just stood there, looking bewildered and lost. They didn't know what to do. "What can we do with all these baby animals?" asked Jimmy.

"We have to find their parents," answered Gram. "The lions can help us."

The lions quickly found their cubs, and it was a happy reunion. They were pleased when Jimmy asked them to help find all the other parents. Shayla said they could go in five different directions gathering lost parents. "Good," replied Jimmy. "Bring them back here." The lions set out to find parents while Daniel, Gram, and Jimmy protected the babies.

As the babies ran around enjoying their newfound freedom, parents started wandering into camp, happy to see their babies. It was very late the next day before the last baby was claimed by a parent. The lions arrived to collect their cubs and say thanks. Daniel had destroyed every cage except the ones holding the poachers.

The remaining cages holding the poachers were loaded onto a flat-bed trailer. Zebras were happy to wear a harness and pull the trailer out of the jungle. Daniel took the lead, and the journey began. Jimmy and Gram walked beside the front zebras, holding on to their harnesses.

Jimmy enjoyed taunting the poachers along the way, asking how they liked being locked up. He knew what he was doing was a form of bullying. It wasn't in his nature to be a bully, but he felt compelled, however, to show a bully what it felt like. He could only hope this would stop them from returning and doing it again.

When they finally reached the nearest town with a constable, people started pointing and laughing at the poachers. The streets were lined with people cheering and clapping. When they reached the constable's office, he walked out and shook Daniel's hand. It seemed they had made everyone happy except the poachers.

Jimmy watched as the constable took the poachers from one cage and put them into another. It was a good feeling knowing he helped bring them to justice. He and Gram were more than happy to help Daniel destroy the last six cages and set the zebras free.

The constable told Jimmy the poachers would be going to jail, and that would keep the animals safe for a little while. Jimmy's only hope was for the poachers to find another way to make money. He thought to himself, *Maybe they will wise up in jail.* But for now, this adventure was over, and it was time to go home.

CHAPTER 7

THE VANISHING UNICORN

Jimmy was getting used to going in and out of the dreamworld and was waking up a little quicker. He was still drained of energy and in need of nourishment, but his mind was clearer. When he woke up this time, all he wanted to do was visit Sioux Z. Unfortunately, he would still have to wait until after breakfast.

While they were eating, Jimmy asked Gram if he could ride Sioux Z before he started chores. She had a better idea and told him to saddle up both horses and they could hitch them to the back of the tractor. There was something she wanted to show him in the woods.

"What is it?" asked Jimmy.

She told him it was a surprise and he would just have to wait.

Jimmy saddled the horses while Gram took the tractor and picked up a big round bale of hay. Both horses were saddled and ready to go when she came driving up on the tractor. The bale spike and hay bale took up the entire back of the tractor, and Jimmy couldn't find anything to tie to. Gram laughed and said, "Looks like you'll have to ride Sioux Z and pull Dragon."

Jimmy jumped on Sioux Z and took off with the two horses, yelling back at Gram, "We'll meet you there." No way was she going to keep up with the horses, so she just set a steady pace and followed. By the time she reached the bottom of the bluff, Jimmy had already walked and cooled the horses down. They were ready to ride some more, but first, she had to deliver a bale of hay to the other horses.

After the hay was delivered and the creek checked and cleared, it was time for Jimmy's surprise. They mounted up and Gram took the lead. They followed a trail through the woods just wide enough for two horses. It was obvious this trail was man-made. When they came to an opening in the middle of a heavy wooded area, Jimmy couldn't believe his eyes.

There was a tree house in every tree that surrounded the open area. Not just a normal tree house, but the entire tree had been turned into a house. A bridge made out of rope connected the tree houses to each other. "Did you build all of this?" asked Jimmy.

"No," answered Gram. "It was here when I purchased the property. Magnificent, isn't it? I call it the tree house village."

"Can we bring sleeping bags and stay at least one night out here?" asked Jimmy.

"Sure we can!" replied Gram. "But for now, let's check some of them out." They spent hours exploring each tree house, finding rustic furniture made from logs in every one of them.

Jimmy thought to himself, *This summer just gets better and better.*

"It's getting late, and we need to go home," said Gram. "We'll bring supplies and stay here tomorrow night."

Jimmy smiled, nodded his head in approval, and started down the ladder. They mounted up and raced home. This time Sioux Z won by a nose. When Jimmy got off Sioux Z to open the gate, Gram got off Dragon and said, "We better walk them from here so they can cool down."

As they were walking the horses, Jimmy asked, "Why didn't you have a horse for yourself before I broke Dragon? You obviously love to ride."

"I used to be just like you and ride every chance I got with Gramps," answered Gram. "After he went to the magic world of dreams, riding alone just wasn't as much fun. Now, I have you, and the second part of my life has just begun."

Jimmy got really excited and asked, "Does that mean I get to stay here and go to school? I don't want to go home!"

"Give it time, Jimmy," replied Gram. "Just give it some time." There was nothing more important to her than keeping Jimmy close at hand. She was working on it, and for now he was here. That was what really mattered. He still had almost two months left at Gram's and planned on using every minute wisely.

After dinner, they sat outside on the porch, making plans to stay in the tree house village. Gram said she would fix breakfast in the morning and then pack enough food to eat while they were gone. Jimmy's job was gathering sleeping bags and pillows. He told Gram he would saddle the horses after breakfast and pack the supplies. It was getting late, and they wanted to get an early start so Jimmy said "Good night."

With the morning came more excitement and a new adventure. This one would not take place in a dreamworld but right here on the farm. The more Jimmy thought about it, the better it sounded. This would give him a chance to put everything he had learned to good use in the real world. He thought to himself, "Maybe I'll even learn something new from Gram."

After breakfast, Gram cleaned the kitchen and Jimmy saddled the horses. He put all the gear behind the saddles. When Gram came out to meet him, he told her they needed a donkey or a mule to carry extra supplies. "We could buy a donkey or a mule," said Gram. "But since we already have horses, why don't you train a couple of them to carry?"

"Good idea," replied Jimmy. "I'll do that while we're down there." They mounted their horses and took off with enough supplies for two days. Gram suggested they ride along the fence row, checking to make sure no wires were down or broken. Jimmy didn't mind. It just meant he could spend a little more time on Sioux Z.

When they got to the bluff, they could see the wires intact all the way to the bottom, but it was much too rocky to risk taking the horses down. Gram said they could ride about three hundred yards east and take a trail down from there. They found the trail and finished checking the fence to the tree line.

They disappeared into the woods, and Gram led them straight to the tree house village. They had already decided which tree house they would be staying in. It was three stories high, with the first level being the living room, the second level a bedroom, and the third level a bedroom. Jimmy had dibs on the top bedroom. He wanted to locate their exact location by reading the stars.

Jimmy tethered the horses and made two more hackamores. He managed to locate enough downed tree limbs to make a small corral. He grabbed the extra hackamores, jumped on Sioux Z, and took off to find the main herd of horses. When they reached the pasture at the edge of the tree line, there they were.

Jimmy leaned forward and whispered in Sioux Z's ear. He told her to pick out the two strongest horses, and she took off. She picked a dapple gray and an appaloosa. They were both large, muscular horses with a wide chest, muscular hindquarters, and a thick neck. He rubbed behind Sioux Z's ears and said they were perfect. He slipped a hackamore over their heads and led them to the tree house village.

Jimmy worked with the horses for about an hour when Gram came out. She told him they needed to make some traps and catch food for dinner. She showed him how to set a box trap to catch a rabbit or a squirrel. She put a wood box on the ground with the open end down. She then tied a piece of string to an eight-inch stick with a fork at one end. Jimmy used the stick to prop up the box.

He picked some fresh clover and placed it in the box for bait. All he had to do was back off, holding the string, and wait. Now, if an animal went after the freshly picked clover, Jimmy would pull the string to remove the stick and the box would drop, trapping the animal inside.

Gram set out to make a couple of snare traps and a fish trap for tomorrow. While she was weaving sticks for the fish trap, she heard

Jimmy making an awful commotion. She went to see what was happening and found him holding a rabbit by the back of the neck. "I can't believe this actually worked!" exclaimed a very excited Jimmy.

"What are you going to do with the rabbit now?" asked Gram.

Jimmy looked at the rabbit, back at Gram, and at the rabbit one more time and said. "I'm not hungry enough to kill anything that looks like Bugs Bunny."

"OK," chuckled Gram. "Let Bugs go." She told him to cross the creek and pick a hatful of gooseberries. "I'll make a cobbler."

When he crossed the creek, he noticed some fairly large trout swimming around. He decided to try some spear fishing. He found just the right-sized limb from a willow tree and made a sharp point on one end. He waded out halfway and stood very still. Before long, a trout swam between his legs, and his lightning-fast hands speared the fish and he pulled it from the water.

This time he remained silent. He wanted to surprise Gram with fish for dinner. He took off his shirt and made a sling to hold the fish and waited for another one. He soon caught another fish and went to pick the gooseberries. He was so proud when he handed the fish to Gram. He could tell she was proud too.

Gram made the cobbler while Jimmy cleaned the fish. He cut some green limbs from the willow tree and soaked them in the creek so they wouldn't burn. When the fish were gutted, descaled, and washed, he placed them on the wet limb and held it over the fire. Gram had already placed a Dutch oven filled with gooseberry cobbler in the fire.

When Jimmy put those fish on the plates, the odor was tantalizing. He had never been fishing, camping, or cooking out, and he had never tasted anything as good as this. Both the fish and the cobbler were excellent. This might not be Mr. Jingle's magic, but it sure was Gram's.

Gram asked Jimmy to gather up the dishes and accompany her to the creek. They both gathered up a handful and started that direction. Jimmy despised washing dishes at home, but this was fun. They got back to camp just as it was getting dark and tossed some more wood on the fire for light.

The rest of the evening was spent around the fire with Gram telling stories about some of her adventures with Gramps. Jimmy was glued to every word because she had a special gift for telling her stories. She made him feel like he was right there in the story with her.

They were having so much fun that they didn't realize how dark it had gotten. Gram told Jimmy to reach in the sack next to him and get two candles out. She pulled a small stick from the fire to light the candles. "We can use these to help find our rooms," said Gram. They said "Good night" and started up the ladder to their tree house.

When Jimmy got to his room, he crawled out of the window and onto the large limb that was holding up the tree house. It was almost at the very top of the tree, and he could see the stars clearly. He was naming the constellations, remembering what was next to what. *Amazing!* he thought. *That direction is east.* And the rest was elementary.

Jimmy woke the next morning to the chirping of a bird. It sounded like the bird was right next to him. When he opened his eyes, he realized it was right next to him. He whistled, attempting to replicate the chirping sound. The bird chirped back. "Cool," said Jimmy. "We're talking. I just wish I knew what we were saying," and he started laughing.

This is the most wonderful place in the world, he thought as he rolled out of bed. All of a sudden, the aroma of bacon caught his attention, and he knew Gram was up and fixing breakfast. He took off down the ladder, ready to get this magnificent day started.

"Good morning," said Gram when Jimmy started down the last rung of ladders. "This is our last day out here. What do you want to do?" asked Gram.

"I would like to learn how to make fish traps," answered Jimmy.

She smiled and replied, "They may not be as fast as your hands, but I guarantee they will catch fish."

They went to the creek and cut an armful of willow limbs. The limbs were a quarter to three-eighths inch in diameter. They stripped the leaves and gently peeled off the bark. Green willow limbs bend easily and can be used to weave furniture and baskets.

Gram taught Jimmy to weave a round basket about twelve inches around and twenty-four inches high. She wove a cone with the top being twelve inches around and the bottom four inches around. When Jimmy finished his basket, she put the cone with the small end down, leaving the large end resting on the top of the basket.

They ripped the bark into fine strips and used it for string to tie the cone to the basket. She had Jimmy place the basket in about two feet of water, with the cone end facing the current. If a fish swam through the cone, it would pass through the four-inch opening into the twelve-inch basket and be trapped.

They went to check the snare traps Gram had set the day before and found two squirrels in the traps. Gram held up the squirrels and said, "Looks like squirrel stew for dinner." Jimmy had never eaten squirrel stew, so he decided to save any comments for later. The rest of the traps were empty.

He got busy training the new horses to ride as well as to pack. The training was going well, and it was getting late in the afternoon, so he went to check his trap at the creek. When he pulled the trap from the water, he was astounded to see he had two fish in his trap. Both fish were just the right size for eating.

Jimmy took the fish to Gram just in case she wanted fish to go with the squirrel stew. When he got to the tree house village, something smelled wonderful. The stew was nearly ready, and Gram had made some corn bread in her Dutch oven.

She thanked Jimmy for the fish and told him to try the stew. If he didn't like it, she would cook him a fish. She handed him a big plate of squirrel stew and a piece corn bread. He took a small bite of the stew, moved it around in his mouth, and started chewing. "This is good," he said and took another bite.

Gram put the fish in the cooler and told Jimmy they'd put them in the freezer when they got home. As they sat out under the stars, Jimmy was naming the constellations and told Gram which direction was east. She already knew, but he wanted to impress her with how much he had learned. She was impressed!

Jimmy's mind had always been in two worlds. The first being the real world, and the second being an imaginary world. Oftentimes, these two worlds would collide, breaking Jimmy's concentration. That's why he couldn't learn and was failing in school.

Thanks to the magic of Mr. Jingles, Jimmy didn't have to drift off from the subject at hand to visit imaginary places. He got to really go there anytime he wanted. Now when it was time to learn, he was able to use every part of his brain to absorb knowledge very quickly.

As wonderful as this tree house village was, they were going home tomorrow and starting their new adventure. Gram told Jimmy to pack only their personal items. They could store the cooking utensils and bedding in the tree house. He was very pleased to leave those things. He really liked this place, and that meant they'd be back.

Early the next morning, Jimmy woke up with chipmunks running across his sleeping bag. He had a good laugh than started packing up to leave. Everything was loaded on the pack horses. Sioux Z and Dragon were saddled, so Jimmy went inside for one last breakfast. They enjoyed a good breakfast, cleaned up, and were headed for home.

They had been home about an hour when everything was checked, cleaned, and put away. It was time to start a new adventure, so Jimmy took Gram's hand and they were off. When they opened their eyes, they found themselves in Fantasyland. "Did you pick this?" asked Gram.

"No," said Jimmy. "But it feels like something is wrong and Mr. Jingles wants us to fix it."

Some fairies came and welcomed them to fantasyland. They were asked to follow the fairies to see the ruler. As they were following the fairies, they couldn't help but notice the hopeless look on everyone's faces. It was as if all the happiness had been drained from them. Jimmy was getting very apprehensive.

They arrived at a small castle about the size of a four-bedroom home. Not what Jimmy was expecting at all, but it was quaint and nice. The ruler stood up and gave Jimmy a big hug. "Thank you for coming," he said. "We have been expecting you." Jimmy and Gram were both flabbergasted with that statement.

"What can we do to help you?" asked Jimmy.

"Catch the vanishing unicorn, of course," answered the ruler. "That's why you're here, isn't it?"

Gram stepped in and said, "Maybe you need to start from the beginning and tell us what's going on!"

The ruler explained how a unicorn appeared in Fantasyland a couple of months ago. It's a magnificent sight to see, and everyone that sees it gets an overwhelming desire to pet it. But when they touch it, it vanishes, taking their dreams with it. Taking away dreams leaves a feeling of hopelessness.

"Who told you we could help?" asked Jimmy.

"Edgar, the greatest wizard of all time," answered the ruler. Gram smiled and asked where Edgar was now. "He said he had to go and could only return if invited. He said you would know what to do," answered the ruler.

"Can you please show us to our rooms?" asked Gram. With that, they were escorted to their rooms.

As soon as the door was closed, Gram said, "We need Edgar." Jimmy took Mr. Jingles out of his pocket and summoned Edgar. They exchanged greetings and got down to business. He explained how the unicorn attracted people and how he vanished. He also told them the unicorn couldn't vanish if he was trapped and held down.

Edgar had already drawn out some plans for a cage to trap the unicorn. It had four walls with a top, but no bottom. Edgar said he could use his magic to levitate the cage, and Jimmy would be the bait that got the unicorn under it. As soon as the cage dropped, Jimmy could hold the unicorn down.

"What makes you think the unicorn will come to Jimmy?" asked Gram.

"Just as the people can't resist petting the unicorn, the unicorn can't resist stealing children's dreams," answered Edgar, and then he said, "Getting him there wasn't the hard part. It would be keeping him there."

They got busy and built the cage to Edgar's specifications and found just the right spot to put it. While Edgar practiced his levitating skills, Gram and Jimmy discussed the dangers involved in this adventure. "Don't worry, Gram, I'll be fine," said Jimmy. Gram gave him a hug and went to watch Edgar.

Back home, Jimmy watched magicians on television levitate objects, and he was awed by it. Russ and Dad always injected their opinions, saying it wasn't magic. It was a trick. They said the magician used wires and ropes with mirrors to trick the eyes.

He thought to himself, "Maybe a wizard is different from a magician." Edgar wasn't using any wires, ropes, or mirrors. He wasn't tricking anyone or their eyes. It was just plain magic. Jimmy snickered with the thought that they were both so wrong. Too bad he would never get to tell them.

Once Edgar got proficient in lifting and dropping the cage, he said, "We're ready, but it's getting late. Let's call it a day and meet back here in the morning. They needed this time anyway to talk about the plan. They would only get one chance, so it had to be done right the first time.

Edgar told Jimmy to reach out like he was going to pet the unicorn. That would be the signal to drop the cage. Instead of petting, Jimmy would grab the unicorn, wrap his arms around its neck, and hold on. The cage would keep the unicorn from vanishing, but only Jimmy's constant contact would make him release captured dreams.

"If the unicorn breaks your grip and manages to escape, he will vanish, taking your dreams with him," said Edgar. "You must hang on with all your might and not let go, understand?" Jimmy didn't say a word. He just nodded his head affirmatively. "When all the dreams have left the unicorn, he will stop fighting," said Edgar.

He continued by saying, "All of the dreams will be gone from the unicorn, even his. You will have the dreams of the unicorn and must decide what to do with them. If you decide to keep his dreams, they will give you his power to vanish. Unfortunately, without his dreams, the unicorn will die taking the last of his kind away forever. If you give him back his dreams, he will never steal again."

Jimmy told Gram and Edgar he needed to take a walk to clear his head and think. As he walked around, he saw some familiar characters from cartoons he had watched back home. Ken and Barbie just slumped in chairs. Mr. and Mrs. Incredible didn't look incredible at all. They looked doleful.

Jimmy tried talking to the lion king but he just sighed. When he saw Snow White sitting on the curb, sobbing, he made up his mind. He went back to his room and announced, "I will do it. This is my adventure, and I will win," said Jimmy. "I will give Snow White back her dreams so she can smile again!"

The next day, the three of them set out to retrieve the dreams being held captive by the unicorn. Edgar raised the cage about twenty feet in the air and hid in the bushes with Gram. Jimmy took his place under the cage and waited patiently for the unicorn to show himself.

Just when Jimmy was about to give up, the unicorn came prancing up to him. This creature was the most beautiful thing Jimmy had ever seen, and he was captivated by it. He shrugged his shoulders and moved his head from side to side to regain full attention. He reached out to pet the unicorn.

Edgar dropped the cage, and Jimmy grabbed the unicorn around the neck. He threw his legs around the unicorn and locked them tightly. He was gripping with every muscle in his body and refused to break hold. The unicorn spun, bucked, jumped, kicked, and could not break Jimmy's grip.

It took a little while, but the unicorn gave up, and Jimmy still had a firm grip. He released his legs and put them on the ground. This was the first time in his adventures that he felt weak. His legs were so wobbly he could barely stand. He finally released the grip with his arms, and they were as weak as his legs.

Edgar and Gram ran up to Jimmy and tried to grab him, but he vanished. "What happened?" asked Gram.

"He has the dreams of the unicorn and the ability to vanish," answered Edgar. Just then, Jimmy reappeared. He was so confused; he knew he was gone but didn't know where he went.

"What just happened to me?" he asked.

Edgar put his arm around Jimmy's shoulder and explained, "You have the dreams and the powers of the unicorn. Now, you have to decide if you want to keep them." He reminded Jimmy how important this decision was and to not make it without a lot of thought.

"I don't feel any different," said Jimmy. "How does this vanishing thing work?"

"It's like any other power. You have to learn to control it," answered Edgar. Just at that moment, Jimmy vanished again. When he reappeared, he was walking away from Edgar. Edgar laughed and said, "I don't think you're in control!"

As Jimmy was walking away, he kept popping in and out. Gram and Edgar were laughing hysterically. Edgar yelled at Jimmy, "Concentrate! You can do it." It wasn't long until he figured out the secret of vanishing at will and not spontaneously.

He was having a lot of fun learning to control the power and sneaking up on people and appearing out of nowhere. He was also enjoying watching the life returning to everyone's faces. He always thought his dreams were a curse, but he now knew that with dreams came hope.

Flowers were blooming, birds were singing, and laughter was heard from every direction. Cinderella kissed Jimmy on the cheek and said, "You'll always be my Prince Charming."

Jimmy blushed, lost control of his newfound power, and disappeared.

With everything back to normal, Fantasyland was exactly how Jimmy imagined it. He was having such a good time, he forgot about the unicorn until they came face-to-face. Once again, Jimmy saw the face of hopelessness. He realized he had a decision to make and needed to make it soon.

He started looking around for Gram and Edgar. By the time he found them, he had made a decision. He said, "I've been bullied most of my life because the bully was stronger. I have the powers of the unicorn because I was stronger. If I keep those powers, I will be the bully. I'm giving them back!"

Gram and Edgar didn't look a bit surprised. They smiled and gave Jimmy a thumbs-up. The three of them set out to find the unicorn. He hadn't moved from the place of capture. He was just standing there, powerless and lost. "The unicorn didn't mean to hurt anyone. He just thought it was a game. He knows now and won't do it again," said Edgar.

"Good," replied Jimmy. "Now, how do I give him back his dreams and powers?"

Edgar said, "Pet the unicorn three times, then hold your hand on the unicorn's head and say, 'Take back your powers and your dreams.' The powers will flow from you to him."

Jimmy could tell when the transfer was complete because the unicorn came alive. He started to prance around with his neck bowed, his mane flowing, and his tail swishing. He was still an extraordinary sight to see but harmless. If he didn't want to be petted, he would still vanish but would leave only with his own dreams.

They were invited to a Fantasyland party to celebrate the return of dreams. Jimmy was the guest of honor. He was completely fascinated with Fantasyland and knew he would return there with Mr. Jingles again someday. This was not where he wanted to go but was sure glad Mr. Jingles took him there.

Jimmy had no idea so many characters lived in Fantasyland. They came by the droves, and all wanted to shake his hand. Cinderella actually arrived in a pumpkin carriage, and her first dance was with Jimmy. The ruler presented Jimmy with a key to the city.

Everything was practically perfect. There was, however, no sign of the unicorn. Jimmy was worried and went to find him. There he was, back at the capture site. Jimmy whispered, "Why are you not at the party?" The unicorn was ashamed and thought he wasn't wanted. "Come with me," said Jimmy.

They went to the party, and Jimmy asked if he could make an announcement. When everyone turned their attention to him, he said, "The mischievous unicorn is gone. Meet the new unicorn." Everyone cheered and Jimmy thought, "Now, everything is perfect."

Just as the party was ending, the sky lit up with the most beautiful fireworks they had ever seen. The fireworks lasted way into the dark hours of the night, and by the time they stopped, almost everyone had gone home. Gram took Jimmy's hand and said, "Time for us to go also," and they started their journey home.

CHAPTER 8

SAVING A DAMSEL IN DISTRESS

When Jimmy awoke this time, not only was he drained; the muscles in his arms and legs were also sore. It was all he could do to drag himself downstairs to check on Gram. There she was, busy fixing breakfast as usual. He wanted to know why he hurt so bad and asked if she hurt too.

"No," answered Gram. "I don't hurt, but I'm not the one that held on to a bucking unicorn." Gram gave him a couple of Tylenol and told him to work off the soreness on Sioux Z. "I've got to tell you, Jimmy," said Gram. "I never would have thought about Fantasyland, but it was a fascinating adventure."

"But that wasn't where I wanted to go," said Jimmy. "That was Mr. Jingles's idea. It seems he thinks my destiny is helping others. That is so ironic because until Mr. Jingles came along, I was the one needing help."

Gram asked, "Are you all right with Mr. Jingles's decision?"

"Sure," answered Jimmy. "I like helping others."

"You've grown so much. We need to go shopping for bigger clothes," said Gram. Jimmy absolutely hated to shop, but his clothes were getting very tight and uncomfortable. He decided that spending the day with Gram would be fine. He knew it would make her happy, and that was important to him.

This was going to be the end of his skinny pants, Aeropostale T-shirts, and tennis shoes. Gram picked out some boot-cut Levi's, snap-down Western shirts, and Justin Boots with a riding heel. After putting a couple pair of Levi's and several shirts in the basket, Gram told him he needed his own saddle.

He picked out a Tex Tan roping saddle and a Royal King bitless training hackamore with reins. As much as he hated shopping, this wasn't so bad. He couldn't wait to get home and try out this new saddle and hackamore. He was sure Sioux Z would approve.

"One more thing," said Gram. "You need a cowboy hat," and they finished off with a Justin Moore straw hat.

"Is that it?" asked Jimmy. "I want to spend some time with Sioux Z before it gets dark!"

"You look like a cowboy to me," answered Gram. "Let's pay for this stuff and go home."

As soon as they arrived home, he ran upstairs to put on his new clothes. He couldn't help noticing how much he had grown. Not just taller, he was more muscular, older, and mature looking. The new clothes were unquestionably more comfortable. He liked the way they looked too but figured a second opinion was needed.

Dressed in his new duds, he went running outside to see what Sioux Z thought. As soon as he stepped out the back door, Sioux Z whinnied and started shaking her head in approval. "I thought you'd like my new look," said Jimmy. "I have something for you as well." He ran and got the new saddle and hackamore for Sioux Z.

After she was saddled up, he jumped in the saddle, and they were off at a full run across the pasture. Now, he not only felt like a cowboy but also looked like one. It took about an hour to circle the pasture and return to the barn. Jimmy took off the new saddle and found just the right spot for it in the tack room. By the time he put a bale of hay in the feeder and filled the water tank, it was dark and he had to say "Good night" to his friend.

After dinner, they went outside to watch the fireflies and listen to the katydids sing. "There's going to be a barn dance in town tomorrow night," said Gram. "We're invited. Do you want to go?"

"I don't know how to dance," replied Jimmy.

Gram laughed and said, "Dancing isn't much different than karate."

He agreed to accompany her to the dance if she would show him some dance steps. They went inside, put on some music, and started dancing. She taught him to waltz and line dance. It wasn't long until

Jimmy had all the steps memorized and was surprised to know he had good rhythm. He figured there was no way he would dance in town, but he sure was having fun at home.

He felt a little better when Gram told him there were no partners in a line dance. Everyone gets on the dance floor and repeats the same steps over and over. He figured he could do that, just as long as he didn't have to hold hands with a girl.

Gram reminded him that he had been there for two months. Time was running out for adventures, so they needed to work together and get all the chores done. That way they could go to the dance tomorrow night and leave for another adventure the next day.

The next morning, they got busy with delivering hay, cleaning the creek, and general maintenance to the farm. They discovered that a tree had fallen on the fence and needed to be removed. Gram cut the tree off the fence with her chainsaw while Jimmy replaced broken boards.

It was a lot of work, but they finished in time to eat dinner and get ready for the dance. When Jimmy came downstairs all dressed up in his new clothes, Gram smiled and whistled. "You sure are a handsome young man," she said. "I'm going to enjoy introducing my grandson to the people of this fine town."

He blushed and put his arm out as a gesture for Gram to join him. She gracefully took his arm, and they were off to the dance. When they got to town, Jimmy noticed he fit right in. As a matter of fact, the boys not dressed like cowboys stood out and looked funny.

Jimmy soon discovered he was no longer a skinny little runt. He was larger than other boys his age. He was even bigger, more muscular, and looked more mature than boys two and three years older than himself. He wasn't a misfit here. As a matter of fact, he had become the center of attention.

He was having such a good time. He was talking to other kids, and nobody bullied or called him names. Then out of the blue, the strangest thing happened. A girl walked between him and the boys. And not just any girl, but the most beautiful girl he had ever laid eyes on.

She was petite, had long blond hair, and the bluest eyes he had ever seen. She made eye contact with him and smiled. His knees got weak, and he nearly fell down. His heart was pounding, and his mouth was paralyzed. All he could do was watch her walk away.

Nothing like this had ever happened to him before, and right now, fighting ninjas seemed easy. As soon as she disappeared out of sight, he regained his composure. The other boys standing around said, "She likes you. She has never liked anyone before."

"Oh, that's silly," replied Jimmy.

Just then, the band started playing some line dance music. When Jimmy saw Gram on the dance floor, he got in line next to her and was dancing like he knew what he was doing. Some of the boys he met earlier joined in, and everyone was dancing, laughing, and clapping their hands.

Jimmy noticed a boy harassing a girl at one of the tables. He looked closer and realized it was the girl with the blond hair and blue eyes he seen earlier. He stopped dancing and went to check on her. She called the boy Mark and said, "No, leave me alone." He wasn't taking no for an answer.

Jimmy stepped between them and said, "She said no, Mark. It's time to move on!" Mark got in Jimmy's face and told him to get lost. "That isn't going to happen," said Jimmy and warned Mark one more time to leave the girl alone. Mark took a swing at Jimmy and missed. The music stopped playing, and everyone watched to see if Jimmy would back down.

He swung at Jimmy again, and Jimmy grabbed his hand, bending it backward against his wrist. Mark was paralyzed with pain and started backing up. When Jimmy let go, Mark took another swing. Jimmy dodged then put his right foot in the middle of Mark's chest, sending him about eight feet backward. He landed flat on his back.

Jimmy was just shaking his head and told Mark one more time, "You need to leave." Mark was a typical bigmouthed bully. He knew he couldn't beat Jimmy, so he threatened to bring back some friends. "No, you won't," said Jimmy. "Go home, cool down, and change your attitude."

Mark left, and the music started playing again. The girl took Jimmy's hand and started to the dance floor. Everyone was patting Jimmy on the back and shaking his hand. It seemed that Mark was well-known as the town bully. He was also the grandson of Mark Wilson, land developer. "That explains it," said Jimmy.

Everyone started dancing, and this time, Jimmy wasn't dancing alone. He was waltzing with the fair-haired beauty he had just rescued from the town bully. The dance ended, and she did a curtsy and said, "Thank you. My name is Kathryn." Jimmy started to tell Kathryn his name, but she interrupted and said, "I know who you are, Jimmy. I asked around before the dance."

Jimmy couldn't believe he had gone from being the victim of a bully to saving others from the same kind of bully. He knew he owed it all to Mr. Jingles, but he couldn't tell anyone about it. So when he was asked, he told them he got his courage from Gram. After all, she was the reason he met Mr. Jingles.

He took Kathryn by the hand and introduced her to Gram. "I'm pleased to meet, you young lady," said Gram. She reminded Jimmy about their early departure in the morning. Jimmy never had a girl pay attention to him before, so this was another new experience, but he assured Gram he would be ready to go when she was.

Jimmy said, "Let's dance," and joined in on the line dance. Everyone was dancing, laughing, and having a good time. The time passed quickly, and Jimmy noticed Gram motioning him to the door. It was time to leave. He told Kathryn that he hoped to see her again and said "Good night."

They talked on the way home about the evening and how Mark was a bully just like his grandfather. "I guess bullies raise their children to be bullies," said Jimmy.

"Yes," answered Gram, "and heroes like you raise their children to be heroes. And speaking of heroes, the whole town is calling you a hero." He just blushed.

As Jimmy was getting ready for bed, he was completely mystified by the events of the evening. He had always dreamed of conquering the bullies and protecting the weak. He never thought for a second, however, that a girl would enter the equation.

After a good night's sleep, both Gram and Jimmy were ready for their next adventure. Jimmy smiled and said, "Let's see where Mr. Jingles takes us this time. They drifted off and awaited their destination. They were, once again, in front of a castle. Not one of medieval times, but one of royalty.

The gates were open, and the people were being summoned to gather in the courtyard. Gram said, "I have a feeling something is wrong."

"Yes, me too," said Jimmy. "Let's go check it out." They crossed the bridge and were entering the courtyard just as the king began to speak.

"My daughter, Princess Talona, has been stolen. She is being held captive by the evil black knight. Nobody has ever beaten this evil knight in combat. I beg of you, however. Please help return my daughter. There is surely at least one brave man willing to fight for her honor."

"I will save the princess," yelled Jimmy. All eyes turned to see who was brave enough to challenge the evil knight.

"Thank you," said the king. "Return my daughter and I will be eternally grateful.

"Are you sure?" asked Gram. "This knight sounds really mean."

"I have to trust Mr. Jingles," said Jimmy. "He wouldn't have sent us here unless he knew we could retrieve the princess."

"Okay," said Gram, "but we need reinforcements." She once again called for Edgar the Great to assist in the battle against the evil knight.

Edgar arrived and brought with him a friend. "This is Matilda," said Edgar. "She's a witch with a great bag of tricks."

Gram and Jimmy welcomed them both and thanked them for coming. Edgar got busy consulting his glass ball for the knight's location while Matilda started making a potion.

Gram and Jimmy set out to talk to the locals and get information about the knight. It appeared that the knight was holding the princess for ransom, but he was asking for more than the king could pay. They also discovered that the knight constantly harassed the locals, causing as much grief as possible.

Nobody knew exactly where the knight lived or how to find him. Jimmy was getting frustrated from a lack of answers. His thoughts got quite loud. "How can I save the princess if I can't find her?"

"Calm down," exclaimed Gram. "Maybe Edgar is having better luck!"

They headed back to see if Edgar or Matilda had better luck then they did. When they found Edgar, he was very excited. "We found him!" confirmed Edgar.

"Fantastic," replied Jimmy. "Do you have a map for me to follow?"

"Not exactly," answered Edgar. "I will need to go with you. The ball will show us the way, but I'm the only one that can read it."

Jimmy wanted to leave immediately, but Edgar said they needed to discuss the method in which to retrieve the princess. "You cannot just barge in and fight such a strong enemy," he told Jimmy. The glass ball would find the knight's weaknesses and show us the best way to beat him.

"We'll leave in the morning," said Jimmy. They sat down and started discussing a plan of attack. It was decided that sword fighting with the knight was out of the question. He was bigger, stronger, and had a longer reach than Jimmy. With the heavy metal gear worn by the knight, hand-to-hand combat would be difficult for him. That was the way Jimmy could defeat him.

Matilda placed a small vial with a potion inside, some bones, and a small sack filled with sand on the table. She said, "Your trail will grow cold three times. The items I have given you will help you find a new clue as to her location. When you lose her trail, think about why you are lost, and you will know which item to use."

Early the next morning, Jimmy, Gram, and Edgar set out to find the princess. Matilda stayed behind to watch after the king. They came upon a small village that was in disarray, and it was obvious that these people had been terrorized. The villagers told Edgar that the evil knight had pillaged and stolen everything of value. He threatened to kill the princess if they fought him.

The knight wasn't trying to cover his tracks. He was so arrogant about bullying people, he didn't even think he needed to hide. That's when Jimmy knew this was the most vicious adversary he would ever encounter. He took Mr. Jingles out of his pocket and held him in the palm of his hand. "Are you sure?" he asked. Mr. Jingles started glowing and blinking. "Let's go," said Jimmy.

Every village they encountered had the same story to tell. "This evil knight is truly evil," said Edgar.

Jimmy's teacher, Mr. Kendall, told the students, "If you look deep enough, you can find good in everyone." Obviously, he never met an evil knight.

Edgar held up his hand to stop the others and said, "We are getting close to finding the princess. But it's getting dark, and I can't see the tracks. We need to camp here." Around midnight, rain started pouring, and water started rising in camp. They scrambled to grab what they could and headed for higher ground.

They found a cave in some rocks and crawled in to get dry. It had stopped raining by the time the sun came up, but all tracks were washed away, and they were lost. Jimmy remembered the words from Matilda, and he took out the three things she had handed him.

He looked around and thought to himself, *Why are we lost? It has nothing to do with bones or sand. It was water, and the potion is made from water.* He took the top off the vial and poured the potion on the ground. It made the dirt turn almost black and formed an arrow pointing north.

They took off in the direction the arrow was pointing and soon picked up the trail again. They had lost some time, but Edgar figured they were still not too far behind the knight. Edgar was in the lead, with Jimmy bringing up the rear. They passed a patch of tall grass, and something caught Jimmy's eye.

He turned to get a better look and realized someone was hiding in the grass. He heard a child whimpering and went to take a better look. It was a small girl, about three years old, and she was injured. Jimmy called out for Gram and Edgar to stop and help.

She told them she was from a nearby village and was attacked by the evil knight. He entered the girl's home and injured both her and her mother. The little girl got away, but her arm was broken. She hid in the tall grass so the evil knight couldn't find her.

Gram set and splinted the girl's arm and noticed she had a fever. "We've got to get her home so she can get medical attention," explained Gram. Edgar and Jimmy chopped down two small trees about half an inch in diameter. They removed all limbs and leaves, making poles. After spreading a blanket on the ground, they put the poles on each side of the blanket and rolled the blanket around the poles.

Gram laid the girl on the blanket, and Edgar picked up the front poles and Jimmy the rear poles. They started toward the girl's village and, unfortunately, the opposite direction from the evil knight. Jimmy wanted desperately to stop this very evil knight but knew the little girl needed them first.

It was almost dark when they reached the child's village. When the villagers saw they were returning the child, they were welcomed with open arms. They were led to a makeshift hospital set up to treat injured villagers. The little girl's mother was being treated at the hospital, and they were reunited.

The rest of the evening was spent helping the villagers put the village back together. They were up very early and ready to search for the princess, but once again, they lost the trail. Jimmy took out the two remaining items Matilda had given him. Sand had nothing to do with getting them lost, but a broken bone did. He tossed the bones on the ground, and they landed in a straight line. "It's that way," shouted Jimmy.

Since they circled back to save the little girl, there was no way they could find and rescue the princess on foot. The villagers rounded up three horses so they could make up lost time. They saddled up and rode off in the directions the bones had sent them.

They were making good time, getting almost close enough to see the princess, when they noticed the sky getting very dark ahead. "What is that?" asked Jimmy.

"It's a hard wind picking up loose sand. Some people call it a sandstorm, and it is very dangerous," answered Edgar.

They jumped off their horses and turned them to face each other. Edgar and Jimmy put blankets over the back end of the horses and secured the bottom to the ground with rocks. All of the remaining blankets were put over the horse's heads, forming a tent. With the three of them standing in the center, they held the horses with one hand and the blankets with the other.

The storm hit hard, and they could feel the sand pounding on the outside, but they were safe under the blankets. It seemed like hours before the storm died down. Their arms were exhausted from holding on to the blankets so tightly. Finally, they were able to throw back the blankets and get some fresh air.

So much sand was moved around by the wind that the entire landscape had changed. Just as Matilda predicted, they were lost for the third time. Jimmy took the pouch holding the sand out of his pocket. He untied the string and poured out the sand. It blew in the wind, forming a hand motioning them to follow it. They jumped on their horses and rode off in the direction the hand was moving.

It wasn't long until they picked up the trail and knew they had to be getting very close. The sun was beating down, causing heat waves to rise up from the sand. They could see something ahead but wasn't exactly sure what it was. At first, they thought it was a mirage caused by the sun but soon realized it was another castle. "That must be the evil knight's home," said Edgar.

Jimmy knew he needed the element of surprise to beat the knight. He entered as quiet as a mouse, and he entered alone. He was clinging to the walls and hiding in the shadows. He moved from one room to another, expecting the worst each time he entered a new room.

He heard voices coming from ahead and stopped to listen. It was the princess begging the knight to let her go. He was tormenting her by mocking every word she said. The princess began to cry, and that made Jimmy angry. He started walking in the direction the sounds were coming from. It wasn't long before he found himself just outside the door where the princess was being held captive.

He put his ear to the door, trying to figure out which side of the room the knight was on. Listening to the princess's cries and the knight's teasing gave him a good idea of their whereabouts. He busted open the door and, without breaking his stride, hit the knight with a running dropkick, knocking him flat on his back.

He didn't give the knight a chance to figure out what had happened before he drew his sword and put it to the knight's neck. "Make a move and it will be your last," warned Jimmy as he motioned for the princess to run. She left the castle, screaming for help. When Gram and Edgar arrived with the princess, Jimmy was still holding the knight down with his sword.

The knight was taken from his castle and laid facedown across the saddle. They used several ropes to secure him to his horse. When the knight was no longer a threat, the princess gave a sigh of relief. She ran over, threw her arms around Jimmy, and kissed him on the cheek. Jimmy started blushing and found himself to be quite speechless.

It took a few seconds to regain his composure and ask the princess if she was all right. "Yes. Thanks to you," she answered. "I have been told you are called Jimmy. I find that to be a strange name, but I am very happy you are here. I am sure we will have a party to celebrate my return. Will you come as my guest?"

Jimmy graciously accepted the offer and helped the princess onto a horse. He and the princess visited all the way back to the castle. Jimmy would take time to occasionally poke the knight and ask if he was comfortable. "What will you do with the evil knight when we reach the castle?" asked the Princess.

"That is for your father to decide," answered Jimmy.

When they came in view of the castle, the guards were shouting, "It's the princess! She is safe!" The gates opened, and the king's guards came riding out to meet them.

As soon as they rode past the gates, the princess cried out, "Father, I'm home." She jumped off her horse and ran to the king.

The king went over and shook Jimmy's hand, and the guards took the evil knight to the dungeon. The king ordered the entire castle to celebrate the princess's return. Jimmy, Gram, and Edgar received special invitations as the guests of honor. They all three accepted the invite.

Since they had some extra time before the party, they decided to tour the castle. They stood and watched the jester entertaining the children and found it quite amusing. They had just turned to walk away when they heard a commotion coming from the other side of the courtyard. As they got closer to the commotion, a man went running past them.

"What's wrong?" asked Jimmy.

The man shouted back, "The evil knight has escaped!"

Just as Jimmy saw the knight, the knight saw Jimmy. They started toward each other. Jimmy spotted a hoe leaning against a tree and grabbed it. He yanked out the handle and said, "Time to practice my kendo."

Jimmy started spinning the hoe handle so fast that the knight couldn't see it. When he came close to Jimmy, the stick knocked him back. The knight shook his head and started toward Jimmy again. Jimmy moved to a ready position and waited for the knight to come closer.

When the knight was just out of arm's reach from Jimmy, he whacked the knight over the head with the stick. The whack addled the knight, and before he could regain his thoughts, Jimmy hit him with a three-punch combination. The knight was still on his feet, coming back for more.

Jimmy used a combination of kicks, starting with a front kick followed by a side thrust kick. He then jumped straight in the air, spinning, and delivered a powerful roundhouse kick to the head. The knight was so addled; he stumbled backward and fell to the ground.

Once again, Jimmy held the knight captive until help arrived. The people were jumping up and down and cheering in the courtyard. Edgar came to Jimmy and said, "Well done, my boy. I'm proud to be part of your family."

Jimmy was feeling quite prideful. Not because he had to fight, but because he made his family proud.

The celebration was still on for the evening, so Jimmy, Gram, and Edgar got ready to go to the party. They met just outside the ballroom and waited in line to be introduced by the doorman. "What if we have to dance? We won't know how to dance like them," said Jimmy.

Gram replied, "Just follow your instincts and you'll do fine."

They stood at the door while the doorman introduced them. He said, "Ladies and gentlemen, I give you Sir Jimmy, the rescuer; Sir Edgar, the wizard; and Lady Sara.

The princess walked up and put out her hand. "Would you care to dance, Sir Jimmy?" she asked.

Jimmy looked around and noticed that they were doing a kind of line dance. Everyone was doing the same steps, only really slow. He watched for a second and took the princess by the hand. They fell in line and started dancing. Jimmy told the princess how similar this dance was to the dance where he was from.

The princess stopped the music and asked for everyone's attention. "Sir Jimmy is going to show us how they dance where he is from." Jimmy went to the band and started tapping out a beat. The band started playing fast enough for a line dance.

He started doing the steps they did back home, and Gram joined in. It wasn't long until the dance floor came alive and laughter was heard all around the castle. Even the king joined in. The rest of the evening was spent eating, dancing, and laughing.

It was a wonderful celebration, but like most parties, it had to end. Jimmy took a few minutes to tell the princess good-bye and wish her good luck in the future. He then took a few extra minutes for Edgar, whom he was becoming quite fond of. He took Gram's hand and said, "I guess it's time to go," and they started their journey home.

CHAPTER 9

RETURNING HOME

Jimmy's journey with Gram was coming to an end, and when he woke up, that was all he could think about. A cloud of sadness was hovering over his head like a bad aura. He headed downstairs to find Gram and overheard a telephone conversation. "Don't worry. I'll have him home in plenty of time for school" was Gram's part of the conversation.

Jimmy didn't want to go home. This was where he was meant to be. He knew, however, that it wasn't his or Gram's decision. At least for now, he had to do what his parents said. He wanted to be a good son, but he needed to be with Gram. He heard Gram crying, and his heart was breaking. He knew he had to make her feel better, so he put on a happy face before walking in the kitchen.

"Good morning," he said as he sat down. "Who were you talking to?"

Gram answered as tears filled her eyes, "Your father. He wants you to come home, but I talked him into two more weeks. Enough time for one more adventure." Jimmy couldn't stand to see Gram cry, so he perked up the conversation.

"If all we have are two weeks," replied Jimmy, "let's make the most of every minute." He asked if he could invite some friends over for a horseback ride and a campout at the tree house village. And he asked if she would mind being a chaperon. Gram was all for it and liked the idea of being the chaperon.

"This calls for a trip to town so I can hook up with my friends," said Jimmy. They ate breakfast and set out to do chores before heading into town. It was getting late by the time they finished their chores, and Gram suggested they gather up Jimmy's friends and eat at a local café.

The first invitation went to Kathryn, and she was thrilled to accept the invite. He really liked three brothers named Brock, Blake, and Boston. He invited them to join the campout, and they were delighted with the invitation. The last two were Marcus and Tiana, a brother and sister he met at the dance. They accepted the invitation as well.

They all gathered at a café called the Country Corner, a small family-owned establishment, popular with the locals. Parents joined in to meet with Gram and Jimmy so they could discuss the particulars of the campout. Everyone, including the parents, was in agreement. The campout was a go as long as Gram was a chaperon.

This was Wednesday, and the plan was to meet on Saturday morning, eight o'clock, at the farm. This gave Jimmy two days to train enough horses for the ride. Early the next morning, he was on Sioux Z, riding like the wind to pick just the right horses. They needed to be smart like Sioux Z and Dragon.

When they spotted the herd, Jimmy told Sioux Z to round out the horses she liked. She took off and started cutting out certain horses. She picked out six of the best mares, and they took off for the ranch. The mares followed Sioux Z into the small pasture by the house, and Jimmy closed the gate.

While Jimmy and Sioux Z rounded up horses, Gram went to town and picked up six new saddles, saddle blankets, and hackamores. When she got home, Jimmy unloaded the new tack and went to work breaking and training horses. He had never worked so hard in his life or enjoyed anything more. He would ride one horse for a while then another.

Gram joined him the next day, and they both worked the horses one after another until all six horses were ready to ride. Now, it was time to gather up sleeping bags and a few groceries. They had decided to survive off the land and catch or trap their food. They packed just the necessities.

They had left cooking utensils, plates, silverware, and cups at the tree house village the last time they were there. Jimmy put everything in the packs he would be putting on the pack horses, and they were ready to go. Here it was, Friday evening, and everything was falling in place. Jimmy was so excited, he could hardly wait for morning.

He was up bright and early Saturday morning, brushing and saddling horses, packing the pack horses, and making sure everything was in order. They grabbed a quick bite to eat, and their guests started arriving. Gram gave the parents a tour of the ranch while Jimmy took his guests to the barn.

The parents left, and the kids were anxious to mount up and ride. They took off at a nice, slow pace, giving the new riders a chance to get used to the saddle. When they reached the tree house village, the kids could hardly believe their eyes. Kathryn said, "This is awesome," and Jimmy was pleased.

Everyone pitched in to unpack the horses and put things away. They each got to pick the tree house they would be staying in. After they laid out their sleeping bags and made themselves at home, they all met in the yard. Jimmy told them to split up in two groups; he would take three and make fish traps while Gram took the others to gather edible plants.

Jimmy was joined by Kathryn, Brock, and Marcus. They went to the creek to collect weeping willow limbs. After cutting a fair-sized pile of limbs, they started weaving and tying until they each had a finished trap. They walked into the water and found just the right places to put their traps.

Meanwhile, Gram took Blake, Boston, and Tiana to pick edible plants for dinner. They found a multitude of wild greens such as bacon, mustard leaves, lamb's-quarter, and poke leaves. They found a good patch of morel mushrooms and picked a basketful. They finished off by digging up some roots of a sassafras tree to make tea.

Tiana asked Gram what sassafras tea tasted like, and she said, "It tastes just like it smells." She took out her pocketknife, and cut off a piece of bark. She told Tiana to take a smell. She smelled the bark, got a surprised look on her face, and said, "It smells like root beer." Both kids got excited and were ready to head back and make the tea.

Jimmy and his group decided to saddle up and ride downstream while waiting on their traps to catch fish. They found a spot where the beavers had built a dam, creating a huge swimming hole. Jimmy took some rope from his saddlebags and climbed up a tree and out on a large limb hanging over the creek. He tied the rope to the limb and tossed the loose end to the kids below.

After tying several knots on their end, Brock held on to the rope, ran back then sideways, jumped up, and put his feet on the bottom knot. He went swinging to the middle of the creek, let go, and made a wild splash down in the creek. He went under for a second, surfaced, and yelled, "That was totally awesome!"

They took turns swinging and splashing for about an hour and decided to head back and find out if their traps had caught any fish. When they pulled the traps out of the water, they discovered all four traps had two or more fish in them. "We've caught plenty of fish for everyone," said Jimmy. They headed back to the tree house village to show Gram how well they had done.

When Jimmy and his group returned to the tree house village, Gram was already there with her group. Everyone started talking at the same time, boasting about their discoveries and achievements. Gram just sat back and smiled. She had learned her survival skills from her Gramps and the magic of Mr. Jingles. These children were learning the same skills from her, and that was magic too.

Everyone pitched in and prepared the fish, fresh greens, and sassafras tea for dinner. It was a delicious meal prepared outside over an open fire. After the meal, Gram surprised everyone with the makings of s'mores for dessert. "I thought we were only going to eat what we caught or found," said Jimmy. "I don't remember catching chocolate, marshmallows, and graham crackers."

"OK, I cheated," said Gram. "So shoot me." Everyone started laughing and agreed the s'mores were the end of a perfect day. Jimmy had always been bullied and never had friends before. It was as if Mr. Jingles and Gram had transformed his entire life. He was so happy here, and the very thought of leaving it made him feel sick.

He kept putting the thoughts of leaving aside and tried to enjoy the moment. He knew, however, that he would have to tell his friends he would be leaving them in a couple of weeks. *Not today and not tomorrow*, he thought. *I will tell them when the campout is over.*

As the evening went on, the guests went to bed one by one until only Gram and Jimmy were left at the campfire. They wanted to enjoy this experience as long as possible. But Jimmy was much too tired to stay awake and also said, "Good night."

The sun was well up the next morning when Jimmy was awakened by the sound of laughter. It was coming from Kathryn's tree house, and he went to investigate. He looked into the open window and was amazed at what he saw. A family of chipmunks was running all around her room. They would run up her arm, across her shoulders, and down the other arm.

When she saw Jimmy looking in the window and smiling, she said, "This is amazing, isn't it?" He just smiled as he watched her laugh and giggle at the chipmunks. He was beginning to think she was pretty amazing herself. That thought made him blush. He decided he had better find Gram and help her fix breakfast for everyone.

The smell of bacon cooking on an open fire brought kids out of their tree houses in a hurry. They gathered around the fire, sniffing the smell of breakfast, and enjoying every minute of the day. Plans were made for everyone to make and set snare traps in the morning and then enjoy lunch back at the tree house village. From there, they would all go to the swimming hole at the creek for the rest of the afternoon.

Making snare traps can be hard work, but everyone was having a good time cutting small trees, making traps, and tying ropes. Gram and Jimmy were the only ones that really knew how to make and use snare traps, but the others were good sports and made traps too. They set their traps and waited to see what would happen.

In the meantime, they headed back to camp for lunch, knowing that the next stop was the swimming hole. As soon as lunch was over, they headed for their horses to saddle up and take off. The entire group had become proficient in saddling their horses, so it didn't take long before they were ready to ride.

It was a beautiful afternoon with the birds singing and the smell of honeysuckle embracing the air. The laughter of children was bouncing off the trees like a mountain echo. Gram wasn't wearing her ten-year-old body from Mr. Jingle's magical world, but she was accepted just the way she was. That made her very happy.

They all spent the next couple of hours swimming and taking turns on the rope, swinging out, and dropping into the water below. Gram was even taking her turns, and every time she splashed down into the creek, it made all the kids laugh. This was another perfect day, just like every other day since Jimmy arrived in Salem.

Swim time was over and it was time to head back and check traps. The kids were having a great time at the swimming hole, but leaving meant riding some more, and they liked that idea too. Anyway, two hours at the swimming hole built a real appetite, and the kids were getting hungry.

As soon as they got back to camp, they all unsaddled their horses and put their gear away before checking their traps. The kids started squealing with excitement and rushing back to camp with the catch of the day. They ended up with three rabbits and two squirrels.

"Gross!" said Marcus. "We're not going to eat those squirrels, are we?" Jimmy started laughing and replied, "Trust me. You haven't eaten anything better than Gram's squirrel stew and corn bread.

"Don't worry," said Gram. "We'll fry up the rabbits tonight and talk about squirrel stew tomorrow."

They all pitched in to help gut and skin the rabbits for dinner. Some were more reluctant than others, but they all managed to get the job done. Reluctant or not, when Gram started frying the rabbit, the kids all grabbed a plate and stood in line to be served. She had fixed biscuits, wild greens, and a big pitcher of sassafras tea to go with it. Everything was delicious.

After dinner, they all sat around the campfire and made up ghost stories in an attempt to scare the others. They begged Gram to tell a story, but she wanted to hear their stories first. As hard as they tried to scare each other, their stories were funnier than they were scary.

Gram finally gave in and started out by saying, "This is a true story, and it happened to my family when I was a little girl. This is what I remember.

"It was during the Depression, and my father got a job on a farm just outside Phoenix, Arizona. Dad had my mother and six kids to take care of, so this job was a godsend.

"The job came with a large farmhouse that was big enough for all of us. It had three bedrooms downstairs and four bedrooms upstairs. It didn't have electricity or indoor plumbing, but for the times, it was a really nice place to stay. That is, until it got dark. What they didn't tell Dad was…the house was haunted.

"The first night in the house, we heard crying coming from upstairs. It was the dreadful cries of a woman weeping for a lost child. Needless to say, we all slept downstairs. We checked everywhere upstairs the next day and found nothing. We convinced ourselves it was our imagination.

"The kitchen had ugly wallpaper with a black background and big yellow flowers. The next evening, when we were eating dinner at the kitchen table, a voice from upstairs said, "I'm going to get rid of that ugly wallpaper."

Mother said, "Go ahead, I don't like it anyway."

"With that being said, the wallpaper started peeling off the wall until not one piece was left intact.

"This happened before dark. and the kitchen was downstairs. Dad jumped up and started to open the door to the outside. The door opened about an inch then slammed shut. Dad tried to open the door again by hitting it with his shoulder. It didn't budge. He told us someone was out there holding the door closed. He hit the door again with everything he had and went flying out the door and fell down.

"He jumped up to see who had been holding the door. Nobody was there. That night, all eight of us slept in the living room with candles burning all around us. Everything was quiet for the whole night, but when we woke up, the kitchen had a new coat of paint and looked beautiful. Our mother tried to lighten the situation by laughing it off. She said at least she and the ghost had similar taste in kitchens.

"The next night, the family decided to at least sleep in the bedrooms downstairs with all the girls in one room, the boys in one room, and Dad and Mother in one room. About midnight, we were awakened by the sound of footsteps running back and forth upstairs."

As Gram was telling the story, the kids were moving closer and closer to her. When she saw that she had them dangling on every word, she blurted out, "All of a sudden, windows started flying open and slamming shut! Every door in the house was opening and slamming shut!"

This was when Gram reached around Jimmy and touched Kathryn on the back of the neck. Kathryn screamed bloody murder, startling the other kids. They all jumped and sent bloodcurdling screams back in Kathryn's direction like a boomerang. Gram started pointing at the kids and laughingly said, "Gotcha."

They all started laughing and begging her to tell another story, but it was getting late. "Hopefully we can do this again, but not right now. It's time for bed," answered Gram. "We have one more day and one night left here. Everyone needs to be thinking about what you want to do tomorrow." She bid them farewell and went to bed.

It really was much later than they usually went to bed, so they slept in the next morning. The sun had been up almost an hour before Jimmy and the others started moving around. Of course, Gram was already up cooking breakfast as usual. She started yelling, "Wake up sleepyheads! Breakfast is ready." It didn't take long before everyone was coming down ladders.

This was more than just breakfast; it was a full-blown discussion on the topic of the day's events. The one thing everyone agreed on was riding horses and going to the swimming hole. That, however, was something to do later in the day. What they needed was a project to keep them busy in the morning.

Jimmy was the one that came up with the perfect plan. "Let's have games and races. We can each plan a game or a race, and we get to make up the rules." Everyone agreed it would be a fun thing to do.

Some went off by themselves while others made plans together. They had thirty minutes to think of something they wanted to do.

Gram was in charge, so she went first. She chose to do a scavenger hunt, and she would give out the rules when the time came. Jimmy chose a gauntlet race. This would take teams of two. Together, they would make a stretcher out of poles and a blanket. After securing one end of the stretcher to the saddle, one person would ride on the stretcher while the other rode the horse.

Kathryn chose to do a three-legged race. Brock chose to do a relay race with two teams. Each team would have two boys and one girl. Blake chose to do a water-balloon toss. Marcus, Boston, and Tiana just wanted to go horseback riding and swimming. Gram laughed and said, "That's fun too."

They decided to do the gauntlet race first. Jimmy chose Kathryn for a partner. Brock chose Blake, and Marcus picked Tiana as a partner. It was decided that Gram and Boston would lay out the race course from the start to finish. Jimmy explained how to make a stretcher. Everyone was handed a hatchet and some rope, and each team got a blanket.

They saddled three horses and tied them to trees at the starting line. When Gram said, "Go!" each team took off together to cut down trees for poles, wrap two sides of the blanket around the poles, and secure the blankets with rope. They ran with the stretcher to their horse and secured one end of the stretcher to the saddle. One person jumped on the stretcher and the other on the horse and took off for the finish line.

Jimmy, Brock, and Marcus were holding on for dear life to the stretchers while Kathryn, Blake, and Tiana were riding the horses. The competition was tight as the horses ran neck and neck and nose to nose. When they crossed the finish line, it was too close to call, and they were all declared winners.

Jimmy, Brock, and Marcus all said the ride was awesome and wanted to do it again. It was, however, time for the three legged race. They decided to keep the same partners, but Marcus wanted to help Gram judge this race. Boston became Tiana's partner and was anxious to be in the race.

The partners stood side by side, and Marcus tied the legs that were touching together. They were given a couple of minutes to decide which leg to start with and who the team leader would be. Leaders were chosen, strategy time was over, and they were at the starting line, waiting for the go signal. Marcus used the traditional start "On your mark, get set, go."

By the time all the games were played and races raced, the day was nearly over. The kids saddled up and took off for the swimming hole. Gram stayed behind to fix dinner. This would be the last night at the tree house village, and Gram couldn't help but feel sad. She did, however, take comfort in knowing everyone had a good time.

The visitors would not be the only ones leaving tomorrow. Gram and Jimmy would be taking their last adventure for the summer. Gram thought of every possible scenario to keep Jimmy here but couldn't persuade his parents to let him stay. She wasn't, however, going to give up. Time was in their favor, and she would think of a way to get him back.

The children returned to camp and finished dinner, and it was bedtime. Every kid out here wanted this adventure to last forever, but not one of them really expected it to. Therefore, they all said "Good night" and went to bed. That is, all but Jimmy. He stayed by the fire a little longer to talk to Gram. He wanted to thank her for giving him this amazing summer. She told him to thank Mr. Jingles. Without him, neither of them would enjoy the adventures.

Early the next morning, everyone scurried around camp, gathering the things that belonged to them. Kathryn kissed Jimmy on the cheek and said, "This has been the best summer ever. See you when school starts!" Jimmy knew it was time. He had to tell his friends he was leaving for home in a couple of days.

He called them all together for one last meeting before they left. Jimmy's friends were almost as sad to hear he was leaving as he was. He assured them that he would be back every chance he got. Kathryn made sure Jimmy took her phone number, and he promised to call her every day. He said his last good-byes, and his friends left for home.

Gram said, "I'll put everything away if you and Sioux Z want to take a ride around the property and make sure everything is fed and watered." Jimmy wanted to take one last look around anyway, so he jumped on Sioux Z and they were gone. He wanted to take a mental picture of everything with him. He thought that maybe it would keep him from missing this place quite so much.

Gram had everything put away by the time Jimmy and Sioux Z arrived back home. Jimmy took off the saddle and bridle so he could brush Sioux Z one last time. He threw his arms around her neck, trying desperately to hold back the tears. "I love you so much and I don't want to leave you, my friend, but I have to go."

Sioux Z gave him a nudge with her nose and started pushing him toward the door. He knew she understood and was telling him it was all right. He put up the saddle and turned one last time to wave good-bye. That's when he saw the tears streaming down Sioux Z's face. He turned around and walked away so she wouldn't see the tears in his eyes.

He went in the house to find Gram. She was holding out her hand. It was time for his last adventure. Jimmy asked, "What's going to happen to Sioux Z when I go home?"

"Don't worry," answered Gram. "We'll put her in the big pasture, and she'll be fine until you come back. I think I'll keep Dragon up here so we can visit Sioux Z every day." That made him feel better, and he was ready to go.

Jimmy took Gram by the hand, and Mr. Jingles carried them away for one last adventure. They woke up on a pirate ship somewhere in the middle of the ocean. The ship was in complete disarray. The crew had run amuck, and mutiny was inevitable. Jimmy heard the cries of a young girl coming from the captain's quarters and turned his ear in that direction to listen.

"Oh, Father, what shall I do?" were the words Jimmy heard. He started in that direction, and Gram followed. When they opened the door, a young girl about twelve years old spun and said, "Go away, please!"

Jimmy put out his hand and told the girl they were there to help.

The man in the bed behind her had died. She told Jimmy it was her father, Captain Ron. The crew was afraid of her father before he became ill. That was why they took orders from him. Now Olaf, second in command, was feared, so they took orders from him. "He wants to kill me and take my father's ship," she cried.

"Don't worry," said Jimmy. "We won't let that happen."

She told them her name was Margaret Sweeney and her father was the captain of a freighter from Switzerland. She continued. "When Father became too ill to fight, Olaf took over and turned the freighter into a pirate ship."

She put her arms around Jimmy's neck and begged him to help her. "I cannot fight Olaf," said Margaret. "He is too big and too strong."

"OK," answered Jimmy. "What can I do to stop him?"

"If you can beat Olaf, the others will follow you," she said. The three of them put their heads together to come up with a plan.

Olaf was bigger and stronger than Margaret, but Jimmy had grown so much during the summer that he was nearly as big as Olaf. Even if Olaf was a little stronger, Jimmy's speed would make him the victor. Jimmy decided he had no choice but to fight Olaf. This would be the first time he ever started a fight and wasn't sure where to begin.

Margaret told them that if Jimmy challenged Olaf to a duel, Olaf would get to pick the weapon of choice and would surely choose the sword. However, if Jimmy taunted Olaf into challenging the duel, Jimmy would pick the weapon of choice.

"Do you think you can bully this Olaf into challenging you to a duel?" asked Gram.

"Sure," answered Jimmy. "I've been bullied by the best of them and know exactly what to do!"

Margaret told them she did not trust the crew. They had been much too eager to turn against her father when he fell ill.

It was agreed that when Jimmy defeated Olaf, the entire crew would be exiled from the ship. Gram told her not to worry. They would get a new crew to sail the ship to port.

The door flew open, and in the doorway stood Olaf. Jimmy moved between Olaf and Margaret. He got in Olaf's face and started poking him in the chest with his finger.

"Who are you, and where did you come from?" asked Olaf.

"Where I came from is not important," answered Jimmy. "You should be asking why I'm here."

"OK, so why are you here?" sneered Olaf.

"I've been sent by the ghost of Captain Ron to protect Margaret from an ugly baboon," answered Jimmy. "Would that ugly baboon be you, by some chance?" Jimmy reached up and slapped the scarf from Olaf's head. Olaf was completely bald on top, so Jimmy pointed at him, laughed, and called him "baldy."

Olaf bent over, picked up the scarf, and slapped Jimmy across the face with it. "On deck, we duel," said Olaf as he was reaching for his sword. "Not so fast," replied Jimmy as he quoted the law of the sea. "It will be me picking the weapon of choice, and I pick hand-to-hand combat."

Olaf wasn't worried. He knew the crew was afraid of him because he was a good fighter—or at least he thought he was. He didn't wait to step out on the deck before he took a swing at Jimmy. Jimmy sidestepped, grabbed Olaf's arm, and flipped him out the door.

Olaf jumped to his feet, shaking his head in disbelief. He ran at Jimmy and once again found himself facedown on the deck. Jimmy said, "Lower the lifeboats and abandon ship, and I will let you go."

That wasn't, however, in Olaf's plans, and he just kept coming at Jimmy.

After almost an hour of taking brutal blows and being thrown repeatedly to the deck, Olaf pulled his sword. One of the crew members tossed Jimmy a sword, and it was exactly like the sword of the ninja. Jimmy was very proficient in this type of weapon, so he still had the upper hand.

Olaf was definitely good with a sword, but Jimmy was better. The hand-to-hand combat had already taken its toll on Olaf. He was hurting, exhausted, and didn't stand a chance. Jimmy knocked the sword from his hand. Olaf tried to recover it, but Jimmy blocked him and the fight was over.

The lifeboats were lowered, and all but one crew member was dropped to the sea below. Jimmy allowed the man that tossed him the sword to remain on the ship. He vowed to always protect Margaret and her ship. Gram asked Mr. Jingles to send all the ancestors to help in getting Margaret's ship to a port.

The ancestors arrived, and it was a happy three days visiting and sailing to the Porto de Aveiro Port off the Portugal coast. Jimmy discovered that sailing was a lot of work, but it was also fun. When they arrived in Portugal, Margaret went about the business of hiring a new crew.

Jimmy, Gram, and their ancestors explored the ports of call in Portugal. Jimmy had never been out of Missouri, and now he was in Portugal. If this summer had to end, at least it was going out with a bang. Margaret was safe with a new crew, the ancestors had returned to wherever they go, and it was time for the last adventure of the summer to end. Jimmy took Gram's hand, and they returned home.

Jimmy woke up the next morning to the sound of birds chirping. *This is it*, he thought. *My last day with Gram and Sioux Z in Salem.* He started downstairs, knowing this was the saddest day of his life. He missed his parents, but not his miserable, little nerdy life he was returning to. He had no idea his life was going to be so dramatically changed.

School would be starting in two days, and Jimmy had grown out of the new clothes Gram had gotten him last month. His last day was spent in town shopping with Gram. He ran into Kathryn and some of the other friends he had made during his visit. This turned out to be a good day, but even good days have to end.

They were headed to the farm for the last time together. Unlike the first trip when they had so much to talk about, this trip was silent. Neither of them could speak without crying, so they said nothing. As soon as they arrived back home, Jimmy went upstairs to pack.

It was nearly dark when he went outside for one last ride on Sioux Z. This time, he would leave her in the big pasture along with all the other horses he had trained this summer. Gram picked him up on the big tractor and let him drive it home. They went in for their last evening together.

Early the next morning, he came downstairs with his suitcases, ready to leave. He loaded his suitcases in the truck and waited for Gram to join him. She came out with a small basket packed with Jimmy's favorite foods for the trip home. He wasn't surprised, because that was just the way she was.

She handed him an envelope with his bus ticket and several hundred dollars in cash. When he took out the ticket, he noticed it was a round-trip ticket, and he smiled. "There's no expiration date," she said. "You can use it anytime from anywhere."

He leaned over, kissed her on the cheek, and said, "I love you, Gram, and I will be back!"

They got in the truck and started to town. Jimmy felt better with that round-trip ticket in his pocket and started reminiscing about the events of this magical summer he spent with Gram and Mr. Jingles. He knew his life would never be the same, but he couldn't help being apprehensive about his future back home.

When they arrived at the bus station, Kathryn and her parents were waiting to tell Jimmy good-bye. Seeing them lightened the situation. They made it easier for Jimmy to get on the bus. Kathryn gave him a big hug and said, "If you need anything, you just have to ask."

Jimmy was still smiling when the bus pulled away. His body was headed home, but his heart would always be in Salem. He slept most of the way home, and this time, there were no demons in his dreams. His fears were gone, thanks to Mr. Jingles. He had no idea if what he had learned over the summer would remain with him. He was, however, about to find out. The bus stopped, and he was home.

He saw his dad and Russ looking for him, so he started walking in their direction. He walked right up to them and realized they didn't recognize him. They were still looking, so he said, "Hi, Dad, I'm home."

His dad had the funniest look on his face and said, "Jimmy, is that you?"

Jimmy started laughing and said, "Don't you even recognize your own son? Help me with my bags."

Jimmy was taller than Russ, and a lot more buff. He was starting to enjoy the moment watching the puzzled look on his brother's face. He picked up one of his bags and tossed it to Russ. Russ dropped the bag, so Jimmy called him a runt and told him to grow some muscle.

"Who are you and what have you done with Jimmy?" asked Russ.

"You mean the dreamer, the nerdy little misfit?" asked Jimmy. He then said, "That would be me." He picked up all four bags and started walking to his father's car. A very puzzled Russ and dad walked behind him. He was actually enjoying tormenting the two of them. He was sure they deserved it for tormenting him for so many years.

Jimmy felt like he was in a car filled with strangers going home—strangers that had nothing to say to each other. The car was silent. When they stopped in the driveway, Russ jumped out of the car and so did Jimmy. They made a mad dash for the living room and jumped over the sofa, reaching for the remote. Jimmy was too fast for Russ and came up victorious.

"Come on, Jimmy," pleaded Russ. "My favorite show is coming on."

Jimmy tossed the remote to Russ and said, "I never wanted the stupid remote, Russ. I just wanted a brother." He walked away and started toward his bedroom to call Gram. She would want to know that he had made it home safe and sound.

Mom stopped and picked up pizza on the way home from work. She was hollering "Dinner!" as she came through the backdoor. Jimmy came downstairs dressed like a cowboy, and Russ asked where his clothes were. "What are you talking about?" asked Jimmy. "These are my clothes!"

"You can't go to school looking like that," said Russ. "The kids will tease you!"

"So what?" answered Jimmy. "I went from kindergarten to fifth grade dressing and acting like everyone else just to fit in. All I ever got was teased, even by my own brother. Now, I dress to please me, and I don't care what anyone says."

With that being said, Jimmy grabbed a piece of pizza and headed for his room. The next morning, Jimmy came downstairs dressed in his Levi's, snap-down Western shirt, cowboy boots, and his straw hat. He was looking proud and smelling like Stetson cologne.

It was back to a buttered piece of toast and a glass of milk for breakfast. He picked up a second piece of toast and smeared some peanut butter on it as he headed out the door. He was at the bus stop before anyone else, so when the bus pulled up, he was first to board. Russ was running late and nearly missed the bus. He was stuck in the front seat while Jimmy was cozy in the very back.

They made it to school, and Jimmy waited for Russ at the front entrance. They started down the hall, and this time, Russ was actually talking to Jimmy like a normal brother. Jimmy felt someone tap him on the shoulder, and he turned to see who it was. It was Austin, and Jimmy's nightmares started coming back.

He took a deep breath, sighed, and said, "Get lost, Austin!"

Austin took a swing at Jimmy. His swing was blocked, and Jimmy grabbed his arm and bent it up behind his back.

"I said get lost," repeated Jimmy.

Two of Austin's friends grabbed Jimmy's arms in an attempt to break his hold on Austin. Jimmy let go of Austin and slammed his buddy's heads together, knocking them down.

Austin was a slow learner and charged at Jimmy in a mad rage. Jimmy sidestepped and knocked Austin to the floor. With Austin face-down, Jimmy pulled his right arm up and bent his hand backward. He put his foot on the back of Austin's neck, pinning him to the floor.

"If I even hear that you're bullying anyone in this school again, I'll be coming after you. Do you understand?" asked Jimmy.

About that time, the principal came around the corner and asked what was going on. Jimmy smiled and said, "Austin fell down and I was just helping him up." He turned to Austin and sneered, "Isn't that right, Austin?

Austin just looked at Jimmy and said, "Right!"

Jimmy helped him to his feet and told him to get lost one last time. Austin took off running down the hall to get away from Jimmy. Russ put his arm on Jimmy's shoulder and remarked, "I guess you're not such a nerd after all."

"Sure I am," replied Jimmy. "I'm a dreamer and a nerd just like Gram and proud of it! It's okay for me to like myself just the way I am. It took a lot of terrific people a very long time to make the perfect me."

THE END

ABOUT THE AUTHOR

Mary White was born in Hollywood, California but moved to a farm on the outskirts of Safford, Arizona as a small child. Growing up in the country without television or neighbor children to play with, she and her siblings entertained each other. Her mother would draw pictures and tell stories that captivated them. She was lucky enough to inherit her gift of drawing and storytelling. Mary didn't take storytelling seriously, until after retiring from a successful career as a paramedic.

After publishing *Jack the Rat and His Funny Little Hat* and *Who's My Friend* for smaller children, she was challenged by some middle school students to write an adventure story for them. This book is for them and she truly hopes they enjoy reading it as much as she enjoyed writing it.

CPSIA information can be obtained
at www.ICGtesting.com
Printed in the USA
FFOW05n0741120716